Dancing with the Viscount

A Howertys Prequel Novella

Emily Morgans

MISCHIEVOUS INK

Copyright © 2025 by Emily Morgans

All rights reserved.

No part of this publication may be reproduced, distributed, or transmitted in any form or by any means, including photocopying, recording, or other electronic or mechanical methods, without the prior written permission of the publisher, except for the use of brief quotations in a book review.

The story, all names, characters, and incidents portrayed in this production are fictitious. No identification with actual persons (living or deceased), places, buildings, and products is intended or should be inferred.

Language: Please note that this book is written in British English, so you will find some extra letters, especially u's (like humour), and a distinct lack of z's (like realise), and while we're at it, some extra c's (like defence). I hope this doesn't put you off an otherwise decent story.

Chapter One

London, England
April 16, 1811

Some say love struck them like a bolt of lightning. For Preston Caldwell, Viscount Leighton, this was not the case. It was rather a slow burn, a subtle encroachment on his heart he hadn't noticed until it was too late. And now his love was irrevocably for one woman and one woman only.

Lady Amelia Warble.

And she was not for him.

She was his best friend's sister, the incomparable beauty of the Season, and hopelessly smitten with another man—a fact she was currently expounding upon with great dramatic flair in his study. The very fact she was there, unchaperoned, could ruin her reputation if anyone discovered their private meeting. There would be whispers among all the *ton's* gossips: a duke's daughter alone with the notorious Viscount Leighton? The scandal sheets would practically write themselves.

The fire in the hearth cast flickering shadows across the walls of his inner sanctum, illuminating the rich mahogany of his desk and the leather-bound books lining the shelves. The air held the scent of aged paper and brandy, a familiar comfort, now strangely interrupted by the whirlwind of a woman who had burst in not long ago in a high temper.

Amelia paced the room, her words a furious tide. The pale blue silk of her gown shimmered in the firelight, the darker sash cinching below her bosom only serving to emphasise the alluring curve of her chest. Each restless movement made the fabric swirl around her legs, and he found himself mesmerised.

He'd watched her dance at countless balls, always maintaining a careful distance, always pretending his interest was merely that of an older brother's friend. But here, in the intimate confines of his study, that practised indifference was harder to maintain.

He shouldn't be enjoying this. Propriety demanded he eject her, but the sight of her—arms flailing, hands gesturing, her dark brown hair escaping its bun in rebellious tendrils—was more intoxicating than any brandy.

If her brother discovered her tête-à-tête with a known rake like Preston—best friend or not—there would be hell to pay. He swirled the amber liquid in his snifter, a wry smile playing on his lips as Amelia's tirade continued. The man she adored couldn't even spare her a glance? The audacity! He smirked. The man must be a complete arse. Or blind.

Taking a sip, he waited for her next bit of ranting when she abruptly stopped before his desk.

"There is nothing to it," she declared, her warm brown eyes meeting his. "You will have to marry me."

The brandy he'd been savouring sprayed onto his desk as he sputtered. "Excuse me?"

"Marry me." Her tone was firm, unwavering.

Ignoring the wild beating of his heart, he stood to his full height, staring down at her. "I think not."

She dismissed his objection with a wave, as if it meant no more than someone declining a cup of tea. "It's a ruse, of course. To make Lord Pensington notice me."

"Marry you? How will that—" He cleared his throat, attempting to regain his composure. "How will pretending to marry me help?"

Amelia rolled her eyes. "Men want what they cannot have. Everyone knows this."

He crossed his arms over his chest. "I do not know this." A sudden unwelcome warmth spread through him as he realised he was, in fact, the epitome of her statement. He couldn't have her, and he definitely wanted her.

Bloody hell.

"Come now, Leighton." Her tone took on a wheedling note as she leaned closer. With her hands resting on his desk, the low neckline of her dress showcased her bosom at a great advantage. He tried not to notice. And failed spectacularly. "It's advantageous for you as well."

"Oh?" He raised an eyebrow, a familiar tactic that usually infuriated her. "How so?"

She straightened, and he instantly missed the view. "You're a rake. A rumoured engagement will improve your prospects. Mothers will believe you're reformed and a suitable husband for their daughters."

He smirked. "Darling, you're forgetting something."

"What?"

"You said it yourself." He leaned forward, his hands mirroring hers on the desk. The proximity sent a jolt of awareness through him as a whiff of her flowery perfume tickled his nose. "I'm a rake. I have no interest in respectability."

With a frustrated huff, she resumed pacing. He circled the desk, leaning back against it, watching her.

"What would your brothers say?" he asked against better judgement. "Would you tell them it's fake?"

She stopped, her eyes widening. "Are you... considering helping me?"

"No." *Maybe.* He shouldn't. He really shouldn't. The thought of being near her, even if it was pretence, was far too appealing.

"Oh, Leighton!" She clapped her hands together, her eyes sparkling with excitement. "Please fake-marry me!"

"Your brothers would kill me," he muttered. "Adrian is my best friend. And Richmond—"

"Adrian is out of town. By the time he returns, I'll be happily engaged to Lord Pensington. Richmond won't even notice. He tends to avoid most social events."

"I have not agreed yet."

Her grin widened. "But you will, won't you?"

Giving her a frustrated glare, he took a long sip from his brandy snifter, needing the burn to counter the fire in his veins. "I doubt your ruse will work," he said. "Pensington is in no rush to marry."

To his knowledge, the Marquess of Pensington was the opposite of in a rush to marry. He was well-respected, wealthy, and considered an honourable man—unlike Preston. He was also quite outspoken about his desire not to marry for quite some time.

They'd been at school together, shared occasional drinks at White's, but lately, Preston had to admit that every mention of the man set his teeth on edge. Especially if the one mentioning him was Amelia.

"It might." She lifted one shoulder in a dainty shrug. "He's not completely oblivious to my existence. We've danced, and he is ever so pleasant. Me being unavailable might spur him on. I'm quite the catch, you know."

There was a mischievous sparkle in her eyes as she made the declaration, but she wasn't wrong. A duke's daughter was a highly desirable prospect for most men of the *ton*. He just wasn't sure the Marquess of Pensington was one of them. Then again, if anyone could change a man's mind about marriage, it would be Amelia.

He'd marry her in a heartbeat.

Averting his eyes from her winsome gaze, he stared down at his boots. The truth was a bitter pill to swallow. Some rake he was, brought down by his best friend's sister. He'd fallen for Amelia last year, during her first season, the realisation dawning when he found himself wanting to throttle any man who so much as looked at her.

This wasn't just lust. This was something far deeper, far more dangerous. He'd spent the last year trying to bury it, to convince himself it was nothing but a passing fancy. But Amelia, with her fiery spirit and undeniable charm, had captured his heart and there was no denying it; he wanted her.

He didn't want her to marry Pensington. Or any other man. He wanted her to marry *him*.

"I'll do it."

It took him a moment to realise he'd said the words out loud, but then Amelia let out a joyous whoop and threw her arms around him. He gripped the edge of the desk to keep himself from embracing her. Or worse. Closing his eyes for a moment, he regretted it instantly; the feel of her warm body pressed against his was overwhelming.

This was everything he wanted but couldn't have—her in his arms, happy, excited about marrying him. But it wasn't real.

Every touch, every moment of closeness would be an exquisite torture, knowing it was all pretence.

Pulling back, she beamed. "Oh, thank you, Leighton! You won't regret it, I promise!"

A wry smile touched his lips. He had a feeling he would indeed regret it. Very much so.

Chapter Two

Amelia tapped her foot to the music as she watched the couples whirling around on the dance floor in Lady Linwood's ballroom. The Season was well underway, and this particular ball had already been declared quite the crush. The dance floor was a mesmerising swirl of colours—pastel silks and rich satins shimmering under the candlelight, moving in perfect time with the music.

The air, thick with the cloying sweetness of hothouse flowers and the sharp tang of French perfume, felt almost suffocating. Lady Linwood, she was certain, was positively giddy with the praise, especially considering this was her first foray into hosting a ball after her marriage last year to Lord Linwood.

Amelia couldn't help the prick of envy. The former Miss Reed had secured herself a match in a single Season when she met Lord Linwood. And here Amelia was—a duke's daughter—still unmarried in her second.

It wasn't even a lack of suitors that plagued her, but rather a deficiency in suitable ones. She found fault in each and every gentleman who presented himself. Too tall. Too short. Too dull. Too... *something*. None felt right. And she wanted whoever she married to feel that above all. *Right.*

In truth, she held an advantage over many other young ladies : a comfortable lack of urgency. Her family was wealthy, her two brothers ensured the line of succession, and she did not risk her father's title falling into the hands of some grasping distant cousin who'd promptly cast her out.

Should she decide to embrace spinsterhood, society might raise an eyebrow, but she wouldn't risk turning into a social pariah nor did she need to worry about the grim spectre of poverty. Her brothers, bless them, would never allow it. Privilege, indeed, was her shield.

But she did wish to marry. To one day have a family of her own. And she had begun to despair of ever finding a gentleman who measured up to her standards. It seemed an impossible task.

Until she met Nathaniel Howerty, the Marquess of Pensington. The man was undeniably handsome—tall, but not towering, possessed a respectable title, a reputation for propriety, and a family said to be lovely.

The few dances they'd shared had revealed him to be intelligent, well-spoken, and in possession of a smile that could make even the most jaded heart flutter. He represented everything she ought to want in a husband, and she had decided she would marry him.

The marquess fit every requirement; he was a sensible choice. He was *right*. He simply had to be. For no one else came close. And she was tired of waiting for a grand passion that might never arrive.

Better to choose wisely than pine away for a romantic ideal. She'd seen what ruin and a bad match could bring, the whispers and scorn endured by women unfortunate enough to find themselves in such a predicament.

Glancing over at the refreshment table, she smiled faintly as she saw the marquess standing next to his friend, Viscount Gowthorpe. They cut striking figures in their perfectly tailored evening clothes, both favouring the popular black.

Good-looking men, certainly, but she would never entertain the thought of trying to charm the viscount. He might possess a captivating charm and a pleasant demeanour, but he also held a reputation as something of a rake. Oh no. She would remain well clear of that particular path to social ruin.

"Target in your sight?"

She nearly jumped out of her skin at the smooth voice so unexpectedly close to her ear. Turning, she smacked Leighton's arm with her fan. "Do not frighten me so!"

He grinned. "Then don't make it so easy. You were too focused on your beau."

"He is not my beau." *Not yet.* Her cheeks heated as she cast another glance across the room at the handsome marquess.

"So, how are we doing this?" Leighton cleared his throat before taking a sip from the glass of punch he'd brought with him.

"Well, I have given it some thought..." She pursed her lips, mentally running through her plan. "We cannot simply declare ourselves engaged. There is the whole issue of my parents' approval to consider—"

Leighton groaned at her comment, clearly finding the prospect tedious. Rolling her eyes at him, she continued. "So you must appear to be courting me for a week or two first. Perhaps three. I have already saved two dances for you on my dance card tonight."

"Brilliant." His tone belied the word, but she decided not to take offence. After all, he was doing her a favour, however reluctantly.

Leaning forward, he turned her dance card over, inspecting it, his gaze lingering on the fact that he was slated for the very next dance. As he straightened, he quirked a dark eyebrow. "You were rather bold, putting me down for an early dance. I rarely arrive before supper."

Snatching her dance card back from between his fingers, she gave him a saccharine smile. "I decided you would not be so ungentlemanly as to leave me alone while my mother and brother are out of town."

He frowned, his gaze momentarily scanning the room. "Who is your chaperone tonight, then?"

She nodded towards the rows of chairs at the back of the room, where her aunt sat half-asleep, a glass of punch precariously balancing on her bosom. "Aunt Ruth is here. Mother is taking the waters in Bath, and my father abhors balls. As does Richmond."

Her eldest brother might very well despise balls even more than their father. They were so alike, in looks and temperament, that when Richmond eventually inherited the dukedom, the *ton* might barely notice the change.

Leighton didn't look impressed. His upper lip curled as if he had smelled something foul. "That is your chaperone?" He scoffed, disbelief lacing his voice. "You could be halfway to Gretna Green with some scoundrel before she even noticed."

His words struck a chord, and she nearly winced as she remembered the mistake she had nearly made in young folly three years ago. Pushing the memory away, she focused on the man in front of her.

"Oh, Leighton! Are you so worried about my safety and reputation?" she crooned, widening her eyes, relishing in his discomfort as he turned back with a scowl. He did not appreciate her humour, but teasing him was far too enjoyable.

"You are not nearly as amusing as you believe yourself to be," he muttered.

"Lies. I am very amusing." She grinned, his only response a huff.

Crossing his arms over his chest, he surveyed the ballroom. "I cannot believe I agreed to this."

"But you did!" She touched his sleeve, his gaze flicking to her hand before he continued to stare at the other guests. "You may not withdraw now. Not after giving me your word."

"I won't." He sighed, his posture relaxing slightly. The music ended, and couples began to disperse. The first notes of the next dance, a lively country dance, filled the room, and he turned to her, giving her a mocking bow. "Would you do me the honour of a dance, Lady Amelia?"

She smirked. "I thought you would never ask."

A low chuckle escaped him. When he led her out onto the floor, she couldn't help but note the subtle shift in the atmosphere. Despite his status as her brother's closest friend, she had never danced with Leighton before. It seemed Adrian had always been careful to keep them apart, no doubt fearing Leighton's rakish reputation.

As they moved through the intricate patterns of the dance, she noted with some surprise that his movements were far more graceful than she had anticipated. He was an excellent partner, attentive and skilled at leading her through the steps. With each touch, each brief moment where their hands met, a peculiar warmth spread through her fingers. How odd. She'd danced with countless gentlemen and never experienced anything like this. It was quite disconcerting.

Despite his initial scowl, it wasn't long before the corners of Leighton's mouth twitched. Who would have thought? The rakish Viscount Leighton found joy in something so simple as a country dance.

"Are you enjoying yourself?" she asked, trying to ignore her quickening pulse as his hand settled at her waist during a turn.

"I am," he admitted, his voice a low murmur.

"And here I thought rakes were all dark and brooding."

He laughed, a rich, vibrant sound that sent an unexpected shiver down her spine. "Can I not be both?"

Pursing her lips, she pretended to consider it, grateful for the fleeting reprieve the dance steps offered. These strange reactions to Leighton were unsettling. "No. I believe those are the rules. Dark and brooding only."

"I will take care to ensure I am not behaving in any manner inappropriate for a rake." His green eyes sparkled with suppressed mirth as he met her gaze, and she nearly missed a step. He caught her, his warm strength steadying her. Something fluttered in her belly. Surely it was merely from the quick pace of the dance.

He is handsome.

Staring straight ahead, she frowned at the unwelcome thought. It wasn't as if she didn't already know that, objectively, Leighton was a handsome man. She'd just never considered herself someone who took notice.

He was her brother's best friend, placing him securely beyond the realm of male beauty she allowed herself to admire. And a rake. Most definitely a rake. Not at all the type of man she wanted to pursue.

She glanced at him again, annoyed at her traitorous eyes as they took in the way his dark hair gleamed under the candlelight, the strong line of his jaw, the grace of his movements. Most definitely not the type of man. No matter how handsome he might be. No matter how determined her heart was to skip a beat when he smiled.

Chapter Three

Preston took another sip of his punch, the cloying sweetness doing little to quench the dry feeling in his throat, while he watched Amelia swirling around on the dance floor. She looked radiant, a vision in pale blue, her laughter bright as she responded to something her dance partner said. The twinkle in her eyes was visible even from this distance, and it caused a strange pang in his chest.

As the daughter of a duke, she was immensely popular, her dance card always full, her hand constantly sought, and it was beyond his comprehension that she felt the need to pursue a particular gentleman. Half the bachelors of the *ton* would happily cut off their right hand to marry her, and yet she seemed intent on the one man, Pensington, who had declared time and again that he had no interest in matrimony.

She never did shy away from a challenge. A wry smile tugged on his lips. Finishing his drink, he set the empty glass aside. He should probably stop drinking. That was neither his first nor second of the evening, and whoever had mixed the punch had not skimped on the liquor. By now, he was feeling quite merry indeed.

The hour was growing late—or early, depending on your perspective—and he had danced twice with Amelia as she had requested, her touch, even in the formal dances, sending a jolt through him.

Her aunt, a matronly woman with a fondness for gossip, had spent the evening either half-asleep or engaged in lively conversation with her friends, paying little heed to her niece. It left him feeling absurdly responsible for his friend's sister, a need to ensure her safety, to shield her from harm, making him unable to keep his gaze from returning to her every few minutes.

That at least was the lie he told himself, even as he knew the truth was far more complicated and considerably more inconvenient.

"Leighton!"

He looked away from the dance floor to see James Grafton, Viscount Gowthorpe and the Marquess of Pensington heading in his direction. As they approached, the viscount, with his perpetually cheerful demeanour, grinned. "Leighton, will you be at White's tomorrow? We need a fourth for cards."

"Yes, I will be there in the evening." He nodded, the thought of escaping the stuffy ballroom to lose money at the card table quite appealing.

"Good. Good." The blond viscount shifted restlessly as he glanced out at the dance floor, giving Preston the distinct sense he was itching to ask something more.

"Was there anything else?" Preston asked casually, a knowing edge to his voice.

Gowthorpe's blue gaze snapped back to his. "I noticed you danced twice with Lady Amelia Warble," he said. "Are you courting her?"

Preston raised an eyebrow. "Two dances is perfectly acceptable." He knew how gossip spread. Had been the subject of it himself in the past, and he could already hear the whispers starting.

"True," the dark-haired marquess joined in with a slight smile, his gaze thoughtful. "But you have never danced twice with any lady before."

"She's Lord Adrian's sister." Preston shrugged, then remembered his promise to Amelia, and the fact that it was his mission to make Pensington think that she might be off the market soon. "But, yes, there might be some interest on my side."

It felt odd saying it out loud. His very own personal secret, uttered as a lie, only it was anything but. An understatement, if anything.

Gowthorpe grinned, clearly amused. "I thought as much."

"I doubt she'll have me," Preston heard himself say, and instantly wanted to kick himself. Why would he admit such a thing? He should not even care. "She's the daughter of a duke and I a mere viscount."

He was a fool, and the liquor was making him careless with his words.

"You never know," Pensington said, with a knowing look in his dark eyes. "They say love is blind."

"What do you know about love?" Gowthorpe scoffed. "You're determined to avoid it."

"Enough to know I want nothing to do with it." Pensington turned to observe the dance floor, the dance having ended and another starting. "I cannot believe I have to attend all the events with my sister. I used to get away with attending one every fortnight, but that will certainly not do now Jessica has had her coming-out ball." The marquess spoke with a heavy sigh, a look of pure dread in his eyes.

Preston couldn't imagine the stress of having to escort a sister around the London Season. The relentless scrutiny, the fear of an unfortunate match or a ruined reputation. He had found it stressful enough half-watching Amelia for just one evening, and the marquess had three sisters. The social pressures seemed immense, but it was not something he ever worried about. His mother wanted him to marry well, of course, but he had avoided her constant pressure without too much difficulty.

"You might find love escorting Jessica to all these balls." Gowthorpe chuckled, enjoying the other man's misery. "I am certain that is what your aunt is hoping for."

"Most likely," the marquess admitted with a wry smile. "I must disappoint Aunt Jane as I have no such plans."

"I doubt you get to choose," Gowthorpe said. "Some marriage-minded mama will set her sights on you and ensure you marry her daughter."

Pensington turned his head to look at them, his nose crinkled in dismay. "You are both bachelors as well. Surely you will wish to steer clear of the fray too?"

Gowthorpe shrugged. "There are a few who send their daughters my way, hoping to catch my attention, as I'm certain Leighton here has too. But you are a marquess, and as such, you are much juicier prey."

"Please do not describe me as 'juicy prey'," the marquess muttered with clear distaste. Gowthorpe wasn't wrong. Pensington was a highly eligible bachelor, with all the duties and expectations that came with his title and rank.

"Just calling it as I see it." Gowthorpe grinned, undeterred by the marquess's obvious aversion.

For what felt like the millionth time that evening, Preston's eyes searched the room for Amelia. Only this time, he did not see her, and a knot of unease tightened in his gut. He frowned. Where could she have gone?

The doors to the garden were open, offering respite from the stuffy heat, and some couples had drifted out for a stroll. She shouldn't have gone by herself. That wasn't safe, and even if he had no real claim to her safety, she felt very much like his responsibility. His heart pounded against his ribs as unwelcome scenarios flashed through his mind. What if she had?

"Please excuse me," he said with a quick bow to the other men. The need to find her overriding any semblance of social decorum.

A moment later, he was walking through the door to the garden, the cool night air a welcome relief after the stifling ballroom, and he stopped to take a deep breath. Couples strolled along the garden paths, their laughter and hushed conversations floating on the breeze. But there was no sign of Amelia, and the unease intensified.

"Leighton!"

He turned his head to see her emerging from the shadows by the edge of the terrace, her pale dress almost glowing in the dim light. A rush of relief flooded him, ridiculous as he knew it was. What did he think had happened, really? She probably had just stepped out to gather her thoughts, not become prey to a kidnapper.

"What are you doing?" he asked, his voice sharper than intended. "You disappeared."

"I wanted a spot of fresh air." She shrugged, the slight shift of her shoulders pulling the silk of her dress across her collarbones. "Now that you're here, would you like to go for a stroll? It seems like the sort of thing someone might do if courting."

"Yes," he agreed wryly while taking in the way her hair caught the moonlight. "If you are planning to sneak away for a kiss."

The idea sent an unexpected rush of heat through him, and he quickly shoved it back into the dark recesses of his mind, where he tried to bury all such thoughts of her.

A light blush stained her cheeks. "Oh. Is that what they are all doing?" She came up to stand next to him by the terrace railing and they watched the blurry shapes of couples moving in the darkened garden. The rustle of fabric, the occasional laugh, could be heard from between the trees.

An image of kissing her, really kissing her, flashed through his mind, but he forced himself to focus on the present, on her question.

"Maybe not all," he allowed. "But certainly quite a few."

A small grin played on her lips. "How scandalous."

"Only if you're caught."

Her gaze flew to his, her eyes wider than usual, and the music from the ball faded for a moment before she pursed her lips. "Do you often take ladies out in the garden for scandalous deeds?" she asked, her tone light, but a flicker of something he couldn't quite place flashed in her eyes.

He frowned, thrown by her question. "Why?"

"You are a rake. Isn't that what you do?" The question sounded innocent enough, but he couldn't escape the feeling she was silently laughing at him.

Deciding to play her game, he nodded slowly. "Occasionally. But a garden during a ball doesn't offer much privacy, so you might steal a kiss at best." He leaned closer, the floral scent of her perfume tickling his nose, filling his senses, and a surge of desire tightened his gut. "I prefer to have my company alone so that I may offer my full attention."

He was playing with fire, and didn't he know it.

Amelia raised her brows. "So you're saying a kiss from you is not enough to convince them of your skills?"

A surprised bark of laughter escaped him. "You are incorrigible, Lady Amelia." He straightened, putting some much-needed distance between them.

Turning around, her back now against the terrace railing, she smiled up at him. "So I'm told. But you did not answer my question."

"Oh, trust me," he drawled, a slow smile pulling at his lips. "Most women I kiss are more than happy to meet me somewhere private later."

Her cheeks darkened as she looked away, feigning interest in the ballroom behind him. He was rather pleased to have flustered her. It did not happen easily. But the words felt hollow now, a reminder of the man he used to be, before Amelia had changed everything.

For a rake, he was quite the disgrace these days—he hadn't so much as looked at another woman since realising his feelings for Amelia. But that was a piece of information he would never share.

"The Marquess of Pensington is watching us," Amelia mumbled, her voice low. "Let us go for a stroll, so he may think you will kiss me." She moved towards the garden path, leaving him with no choice but to follow.

He groaned inwardly. There might be others walking the gardens, but he did not relish the idea of walking in the dark with Amelia. The carefully planned paths, meant to provide the illusion of privacy while maintaining propriety, were lit by lanterns hanging from the apple trees. Still, there were plenty of dark corners where couples could slip away from watchful eyes.

A proper gentleman would maintain a respectable distance, ensure their path kept them in sight of the house. Instead, he found himself wanting to pull her into those shadows and steal a kiss he could never have.

He never should have agreed to this charade. He was losing all sense of propriety, all the carefully constructed reasons he had to remind himself why he should stay away from Amelia.

Even pretending to still be the rake he was known for was a way to keep her at bay, but now his actions were leading him straight to the fire. He was such a fool. Especially since Pensington seemed intent on remaining a bachelor, and it was all in vain.

"Leighton?" Amelia's soft voice cut through his thoughts, and he smiled wryly.

"If we are meant to be courting," he said slowly. "Perhaps it is time for you to address me by my given name." It was dangerous territory, but he seemed powerless to stop himself from walking further down the path to hell.

"Really, we should not do so until engaged," she pointed out, but a smile tugged at the corners of her mouth. "However, I am more than happy to call you by your first name in private. And you may use mine, of course."

"Thank you, *Amelia*." He winked at her, and the hint of a smile blossomed into a full-blown grin.

"So, will you go for a stroll with me, *Preston*?"

He had not expected to feel so affected by her uttering his name, but he loved the way it sounded, a melody that was all his. Silently, he offered her his arm and she took it. The light touch of her hand on him was enough to make him want to drag her into one of those dark corners of the garden and show her exactly how good his kissing was, to feel her lips on his, to feel her in his arms and... He was spiralling.

This had been a terrible idea.

Chapter Four

A light breeze, carrying the scent of damp earth and blooming roses, sent a lock of hair tumbling across Amelia's face, tickling her nose. Pushing it back, she glanced up at Leighton—*no, Preston*—as they ambled through the darkened garden, her hand resting lightly on his arm.

While the strategically placed hanging lanterns offered pools of soft light, the darkness reigned where their flames couldn't reach. It felt almost like a different world out here, a clandestine escape from the relentless crush of the ballroom with the hushed whispers and rustling fabrics of other couples surrounding them. Some she couldn't even see. A world of secrets and stolen moments.

"I've never been out in the garden during a ball before," she admitted, the words barely a whisper, as if she were sharing a forbidden confidence.

Preston scoffed softly, the sound laced with a hint of amusement. "I certainly hope so. Your reputation is far too important to risk it."

It was true. She'd never ventured further outside than a balcony or terrace until now, not wanting to risk her hard-won reputation by going for a stroll with a gentleman, much less into the darkened depths of the garden. Preston's response, however, sparked her playful nature.

Gripping his arm a little tighter, she tilted her head, looking up at his profile in the semi-darkness, trying to read his emotions in his shadowed face. "It feels almost forbidden, doesn't it? Like anything could happen out here."

The narrowing of his eyes and the slight tightening of his jaw implied he did not care for the direction of their conversation.

"You should never allow a gentleman to take you into a garden unless you're prepared for him trying to steal a kiss. Which, if witnessed, could be utterly devastating for your reputation," he warned, his tone edged with something that sounded suspiciously like concern.

"Not every man would take liberties simply because a lady agrees to take the air," she scoffed, rolling her eyes at his pronouncement.

"You'd be surprised." Preston turned his head to look at her, his gaze lingering a moment longer than was proper. "Do not risk it, Amelia. You are the daughter of a duke. The scandal would quickly travel through all of London, faster than you can imagine, and it could ruin you. Your life would never be the same."

"True," she conceded with a slight smile. "But because I am the daughter of a duke, once safely married, no one would dare say another word about it."

"Just—" He cut himself short, letting out a frustrated sigh. "Just be careful. I know you have your sights set on Pensington, but you shouldn't even walk like this with him if you wish to remain safe. He's an honourable man and would do nothing to risk your reputation, but he's also rather popular among the ladies. All it takes is one vicious rumour from a jealous rival, and your reputation will be irrevocably tarnished."

"That seems rather unfair." She pursed her lips, deep in thought. "What if I wanted Pensington to kiss me? Then can I join him for a walk in a dark garden?"

"No!"

The vehemence of the exclamation made her jump, her hand tightening on his arm as she turned to stare at him. He wasn't looking at her, his gaze fixed on a couple further down the path, the strain in his features palpable.

Glancing at her, he cleared his throat and visibly relaxed, though she could still see the tension in his jaw. "As I said, you shouldn't join anyone out here, ideally."

She couldn't resist a teasing grin, the urge to provoke him too strong to deny. "But I am out here with you right now." Taking his arm in both of her hands, she tugged him towards the shadows. "And I like it. It feels very..." She searched for the right word. "Private."

Looking around, she made sure no one was watching them before she slipped in between the trees, into a darkened section of the garden, then turned to see Preston glaring after her.

"Brilliant," he muttered under his breath, clearly annoyed. A quick glance around, before he reluctantly stepped into the relative darkness beside her. "What are you playing at? If anyone catches us like this, there will be hell to pay." His voice was a low growl in the shadows.

She chuckled, enjoying his obvious discomfiture. "Then maybe you shouldn't have followed me."

"Yes," he replied sarcastically, "because it would have made much more sense for people to see me standing there, talking to a tree."

He glanced back at the path, then back at her.

"Are you worried about your reputation?" she teased, knowing full well it wasn't his reputation he cared for.

He took a step closer, his tall form filling the small space, and she realised just how intimate it felt. She could see little but his outline against the lighter path on the other side of the trees, the scent of sandalwood surrounding her as he leaned down, his breath a warm caress against her ear. The familiar scent, one she had caught hints of during their dances, seemed more potent here in the darkness, making her pulse quicken traitorously.

Suddenly, he was no longer the safe, familiar friend of her brother, but a man of flesh and blood. A very handsome one that sent goosebumps across her skin.

"I am not worried about my reputation," he said, his voice a low rumble. "But you ought to be. You are currently hiding in the garden with a rake."

She scoffed, but didn't feel quite as confident as she pretended. It was one thing to tease, another entirely to admit that her heart was pounding against her ribs. Not that she thought Preston would ever do anything against her will. Or at all, really. He had shown no interest in her. Always aloof, treating her as his friend's annoying little sister. Which, she supposed, she was.

"You may be a rake," she said, her voice barely above a whisper, "but we both know you would never risk my reputation."

"I am risking your reputation right now, Amelia." His tone was even, but she still felt the weight of his words.

"That's not what I meant." She huffed, irritated by his refusal to engage properly. "I mean, you would never kiss me. In fact, I doubt you'd ever consider it."

He pulled back, straightening to his full height. "What makes you say that?"

If only she could see his eyes, she would understand him better. There was a quality to his voice that she couldn't place, and the darkness only amplified her confusion.

She lifted a shoulder in a careless shrug, hoping to sound nonchalant. "Well... you are Adrian's best friend. Naturally, you would never risk your friendship with him, nor the wrath of my father and Richmond. Also, I suspect I'm not your type. You have never shown any interest beyond indulgence when I tried to join you and Adrian in your activities."

A sharp bark of laughter interrupted her, and she scowled at him. "What is so amusing?"

He shook his head, still chuckling softly, the sound warm in the night air. "Nothing, Amelia. It's nothing."

"I do not appreciate being laughed at." Her indignation was real, her pride pricked by his reaction.

There was a glint of what she suspected were his teeth in the dim light. "I wasn't laughing at you. And besides, you jest, tease, and act the fool far too much to not enjoy being laughed at."

"Not the same," she muttered, still rankled by his laughter. It was one thing to have people laughing at her when she was trying to be amusing, quite another when she was only stating the truth.

"Fair enough." His voice was a low caress in the darkness, soothing her ruffled feathers and sending an unexpected shiver through her body.

She crossed her arms over her chest, her gaze fixed on the shadowed planes of his face. "So, will you tell me what you found so amusing?"

Silence greeted her question, and he shifted from one foot to the other, his movements restless, as if he were a caged animal. A shadowy arm came up to scratch at the hair behind his ear as he turned slightly to glance out into the garden. Was he looking for an escape? Or ensuring no one was close?

"Preston?"

His name made him turn back to her. "It matters little, Amelia," he said. "It merely surprised me that is how you see me."

"As my brother's friend?" How else would she see him?

Another moment of silence, then a quiet, "Yes."

What was he not telling her? She didn't enjoy being left in the dark, especially by someone she considered a friend. "Am I so wrong in judging your character?" she asked, pushing for answers. "Am I to believe you are rake enough to compromise your best friend's sister?"

"Of course not!" He stepped closer to her, his frustration clear in his every movement, the hand that had been in his hair now falling to his side, his fingers curled into a fist. "I would never risk your reputation."

She tilted her head, staring at him in the darkness, her heart pounding against her ribs, making her breath shallow. "Then what?"

Another step, bringing them indecently close in the small space between the trees, and she held her breath. For a moment, she thought he might lean down and kiss her, though she couldn't fathom where the idea came from. Preston may be a rake, but she was far from the type of woman he usually went for.

"Why are you still unmarried?" His question surprised her.

"No one has caught my interest," she said, annoyed to hear the tremor in her voice. "I could have sworn I told you this.

None of my suitors have been someone I could envision myself spending the rest of my life with."

The thought of a life with someone that did not spark at least something in her seemed like a bleak existence, and then she'd rather remain alone.

"But you can with Pensington?" Preston's low murmur almost sounded like a challenge.

She nodded, even though she knew it was all a dream she had created for herself. The marquess did not know her, and she did not know him. Not truly. But he was the only one she had not wanted to dismiss immediately.

Other than possibly Preston.

She pushed the unbidden thought away, her mind a whirlwind of confusion. It wasn't something she had ever considered. Preston was Adrian's friend. Preston usually found her a nuisance. Preston stood far too close to her in the dark...

"Why have *you* not married?" she asked, cursing the breathlessness of her voice. She had not expected to be so affected by him, by their nearness.

"I..." He raked a hand through his hair, the action a sharp, frustrated motion in the stillness. "I will one day, but I am in no rush."

Why did she feel like he was lying? Or at the very least, hiding something from her?

"So no young lady has caught your interest?" she teased, trying to regain some semblance of control. "You are no better than I am."

"At least I have not set my sights on an unsuspecting target intending to make them mine." His voice held a sharp edge she had not heard before.

She huffed, offended by the implication. "It's not as if I can force Lord Pensington if he does not wish to marry me. I am not a fool, Preston. I want him to court me so I can see if we might be a good fit. If not, I will obviously not push forward with it. But he is the only suitable gentleman that I feel remotely interests me. And currently, he has shown no interest... Hence me asking for your help."

She refused to apologise for what she wanted.

Preston looked ready to say something. He even raised his hand to her, his fingers outstretched, as if to touch her. Then he let it fall to his side, a defeated sigh escaping him. "Very well. I shall do my very best to act the lovesick puppy, following you to make the marquess jealous. All for you, Amelia."

She scowled at him, even though she was fairly sure he couldn't see it. "If you truly do not wish to help me, then you may stop."

"Really?" he drawled, a hint of something dark in his tone. "That is not the impression you've been giving me. I thought I was locked in by this promise, a prisoner in your little game."

Annoyed by his reticence, his infuriating ability to unsettle her, she pushed past him, needing to escape. "Fine!" she snapped, turning away. "You are released from your promise!"

His hand shot out and caught her arm, pulling her back towards him with a force that stole her breath. He towered over her, his body so close she could feel the heat of him, and her breathing became shallow.

"I will do it," he growled. "I will do my best to see you find your happily ever after with Pensington, but don't expect me to act happy about it." His grip on her arm tightened.

"Why not?" she breathed, the question barely audible as her heart beat a frantic rhythm against her ribs.

As he leaned closer still, she thought she might have stopped breathing altogether. Silence stretched out between them as they looked at each other in the darkness. With a frustrated grunt, he finally stepped back, releasing her arm as if he had been burned.

"Go back inside," he said, his tone curt, almost rude. "Before we are discovered, and you are forced to marry the wrong person."

For a moment, she could do little but stare at the dark shadow in front of her. Then she turned on her heel and hurried back to the ballroom, her mind reeling, and her body trembling. What had just happened? Had Preston been about to kiss her? Even worse, did she *want* him to kiss her? That she wasn't sure which prospect frightened her more—his almost-kiss or her desire for it—was perhaps the most terrifying thing of all.

Chapter Five

The muted sounds of conversation, the soft rustle of papers being turned, and the click of billiard balls did nothing to improve Preston's mood as he sat at White's two days later.

The revelation of exactly how Amelia saw him had burrowed under his skin, an unwelcome and festering wound. As her brother's friend. Someone who, at best, tolerated her presence.

She could not be more wrong.

If he appeared aloof and detached around her, it was only because he was trying so hard to hide his true feelings. To conceal the desire that burned for her with a terrifying intensity. How much he wanted her, in every way that a man could want a woman.

It probably shouldn't have surprised him. She had never given him any indication she thought of him as anything other than Adrian's friend. And yet... on some foolish, irrational level, he had harboured a desperate hope that she did.

It was a dangerous game he played with himself, one he tried to quench at every turn. He knew he was not for her, that his feelings were an inconvenient complication she neither wanted nor deserved. But that bitter knowledge was not enough to extinguish his feelings completely. If anything, it only seemed to stoke them further.

Playing the role of someone besotted with her—courting her—felt a little too real, a dangerous line he was teetering on. He should never have agreed to this farce, this self-inflicted torment. Being with her, pretending an interest he actually felt, was agony.

In the garden the other night, he'd been so damn close to leaning down and kissing her, so close to revealing the true depth of his feelings, before the last shred of common sense had kicked in. She did not want him. She wanted bloody Pensington.

"Leighton."

He looked up, his mood instantly darkening as he found Adam Warble, the Marquess of Richmond and the future Duke of Hoyton, staring down at him, his expression unreadable. He might be titled as marquess now, but soon he'd be a duke and would certainly find Preston an unsuitable match for his sister.

"Richmond." He nodded curtly in greeting as the other man sat down next to him, his movements stiff and formal. Amelia's oldest brother shared her dark brown hair, but his eyes were a light blue rather than the warm brown of his sister's. He also lacked her playful nature, taking after their severe father. "Any news from Adrian?"

The marquess lifted a shoulder in a shrug, a movement not entirely unlike the one Amelia often employed, sending a jolt of unexpected longing through him.

"He sent word that he should be back in another fortnight. Mother is enjoying his company far too much to allow him to return to London quite yet. He reckons he will bore her by then." Richmond's pale blue eyes turned to Preston, cold and piercing. "I hear you've been seen hovering around Amelia lately."

It wasn't a question. It was a veiled threat. Keeping his voice even, Preston nodded, trying to appear nonchalant. "Yes. I've been keeping an eye on her with Adrian away. He usually is the one to watch out for her, to ensure no harm comes to her."

"Ah, yes. My father and I care little for the social scene." Richmond took a sip of his drink, his tone bored. "Our aunt is her chaperone, so don't feel obliged to step into my brother's shoes. Or try to take advantage."

"Not at all. I am enjoying her company." The words were out before he could stop them, and he cursed himself as the other man's eyes narrowed. He was being far too obvious.

"As long as you do not enjoy her company too much." Richmond's words were clipped and precise, like a warning. A warning he should heed.

How did Amelia think their pretend courtship would go down with her family? They would definitely expect more than a viscount. Preston might be from an old family, but he was still only a viscount.

A duke's daughter would easily catch the interest of a marquess or earl at the very least. He was no match for her in society's eyes, something Richmond's cold stare made painfully clear. And yet, he wanted her with an intensity that terrified him.

"Of course," he muttered, forcing a smile he didn't feel. "Wouldn't dream of it."

That was a blatant lie. His dreams were filled with Amelia, with her laughter, her touch, the scent of her perfume. But he'd never share such intimate details, not with anyone, certainly not with her overprotective older brother.

He suppressed a groan. What a bloody mess this was. Standing abruptly, he sketched a curt bow and excused himself. He had better things to do than be scrutinised by Richmond, who seemed to be able to see straight into his soul. Or at the very least, straight into his wicked heart.

When he entered his home a short while later, his butler approached him within moments, his white brows drawn together, his expression unusually severe.

"My Lord," he said with a bow, his tone disapproving. "Lady Amelia is waiting for you in the reception room."

"Splendid." There was no hiding the sarcasm in his voice, but his butler's face didn't so much as twitch. Giving him his hat,

Preston moved towards the reception room, a sense of unease creeping through him. "Thank you, Giles."

Amelia looked up as he entered, her face lighting up with a radiant smile that punched right through him, his heart clenching painfully. "Good afternoon! Where have you been? I have waited forever."

Her impatience was oddly charming, even as he dreaded finding out why she had sought him out at home. Again.

"Good afternoon, Amelia." He stopped just inside the door, keeping as much distance as he could between them. "What are you doing here?"

"I thought perhaps you could accompany me for a ride in Hyde Park. It seems like the type of thing a courting couple might do." Her words were delivered with a lightness that contrasted the storm he carried within.

He frowned, his thoughts going straight to the image of her being seen with a rake. "Could you not have sent me a note about this? You really must stop visiting me at home, Amelia. It is highly irregular and could cause a scandal."

"Oh, posh!" She swatted his rebuke away with a wave of her hand, her dismissive tone making him want to both laugh and groan. "I even have a chaperone with me."

After a long, elaborate look around the room, his gaze returned to hers, his brow raised in question. They were most definitely alone.

"Well, my lady's maid went off to meet some friend of hers who apparently works here." She grinned, the mischievous glint in her eyes a sign of her troublemaking. "Are you not going to offer me tea?"

"I thought we were going for a ride in Hyde Park?" He was losing his mind, and she was the cause.

When her grin widened, he realised he'd been utterly outmanoeuvred. She had led him into her trap, and he had to commend her deviousness.

"Well played." A wry smile tugged at his lips. "I will ask them to prepare my curricle."

Her victorious grin followed him as he called for a servant and made the request, feeling a mix of exasperation and a reluctant admiration. He had to admit that he had missed seeing that smile.

"I do not know why you are so pleased," he said as he sank down on a settee, still careful to keep a reasonable distance between them. "Shouldn't you be chasing a ride with Pensington? I thought that was the goal of all this foolishness."

"Perhaps," she agreed, her eyes sparkling. "I thought perhaps I will try to befriend his sister. I hear she is out this Season."

"I believe so." He groaned, trying to suppress the feeling of jealousy that had gripped him at the mere idea of her spending time with the marquess. "Do you not think that it is rather mercenary of you to befriend someone for such selfish reasons?"

She rolled her eyes as if he'd said the silliest thing. "I will only be her friend if we actually make a connection. Believe it or not, Preston, I am not completely without heart."

He knew she wasn't. He just wished it wasn't quite so set on a man who wasn't him.

"Oh!" He nearly jumped as Amelia clapped her hands together, her enthusiasm bubbling over. "You should court her! Then, as your friend, I can attend events with her and the marquess."

Her casual way of manipulating him was infuriating, and yet, somehow, he still found it endearing. He had to be completely mad.

"You already attend plenty of events with the marquess," he pointed out sardonically.

"More private ones," she clarified, her eyes twinkling. "You know, private tea invitations and dinners. That sort of thing."

Straightening where he sat, he ran a hand through his hair, feeling the beginnings of a headache creeping in. "I thought I was courting *you*," he grumbled. "Make up your mind, Amelia."

She stood, her movements animated as she flitted across the room with excited energy, completely oblivious to his inner turmoil. "Yes, yes. Of course. But if this leads nowhere, I think that is a brilliant option."

He did not agree. Lady Jessica Howerty, Pensington's sister, was probably a fine woman, but he had no interest in getting to know her any better. His heart, that stubborn, traitorous muscle, had already made its choice.

Ever the fool, he had no interest in anyone beyond Amelia, and while he could not have her, he would pursue no one else either, not if he could help it. At least, not for the time being.

He supposed, eventually, he might have to find himself a wife, someone suitable, but there was no rush. Plenty of time for him still to wish for what he could not have. A fool, indeed.

When a footman came to inform them that the curricle was ready, he was rather relieved to abandon the topic of Pensington's sister. Escorting Amelia outside, he assisted her into the vehicle before following himself, and being handed the reins by a groom.

The sun warmed their faces as he nudged the horses into motion. Amelia tilted her head up, her skin glowing with the warmth, and he found himself, against his better judgement, noticing just how beautiful she was.

"It is such a lovely day," she said, looking not entirely unlike a cat languishing in a spot of sunlight, her eyes closed, her expression serene.

He grunted in reply, not trusting himself to look too closely at his beautiful travel companion. The bonnet she'd donned hid most of her hair, but the few loose curls framing her face glowed golden brown in the sun. Her long, dark eyelashes rested against her cheeks as she basked in the warmth, the image searing itself into his memory.

A slight smile lingered on her soft-looking lips. He was definitely not wondering how they would taste if he captured them in a passionate kiss. Definitely didn't imagine her sighing as he pulled her lithe body against his own. These forbidden thoughts were becoming harder to suppress with each passing day.

Hell. He had to stop this.

Staring straight ahead, he forced himself to loosen his grip on the reins, as he was white-knuckling the leather. Not looking at her wasn't helping nearly as much as he'd hoped, because he could still feel the heat of her body as her thigh and hip rested next to his on the seat, her light flowery scent never quite leaving him.

Bloody hell, he needed this sham courtship to finish before... before what? Before his resolve snapped and he kissed her? He would never do that. He would never risk her reputation. It was far too dangerous a game when he doubted his ability to leave it at one kiss.

One kiss would never be enough, not when he longed for a lifetime of them.

He scoffed, the sound sharp and bitter in the warm air. This infatuation with Amelia was turning him into a lovesick fool. Adrian would laugh himself breathless if he knew a woman had brought his rakish friend to his knees. Well, as long as he did not know it was his sister.

"What is the matter?" Amelia's voice broke through his thoughts, her brow furrowed in concern. "You look like you've smelled something foul."

"No, I..." Tilting his head, he gave her a teasing smile, forcing himself out of the dark mood she had inadvertently put him in. "I didn't want to say anything, but did you forget to bathe as of late?"

She gasped, her eyes widening, and she hit him in the arm even as she was laughing, her hand lingering a little too long. "How dare you suggest I stink!"

Grinning, he shrugged, enjoying her playful outrage. "You are the one who brought up foul-smelling things."

"Perhaps you are the one who smells." Her nose wrinkled in mock disgust.

"I'll have you know I am newly bathed and smell amazing." He pretended to give her a superior look, but nearly choked on his own laughter as she leaned in to smell him, her actions sending his carefully constructed calm spiralling into chaos.

Her nose briefly touched his neck, and the jolt of awareness the skin to skin contact elicited sent shivers through his body, making him sit as straight as a rod, his grip tightening on the reins.

"You do smell nice," she said with an amused smile as she pulled back, her eyes sparkling with laughter.

"Amelia," he croaked, his voice raspy. This unsolicited and unwanted desire had to be reined in before it got out of control. Clearing his throat, he continued, "You cannot do that. If someone saw you that close to me, it would be a scandal."

"If anyone heard us speaking of bathing, it would be a scandal." Her mischievous grin returned. "We've known each other too long to worry about these things, Preston. We are not in Hyde Park yet, and no one on the street saw us. And no one can hear us. We can discuss anything we like."

"Maybe not anything," he muttered, his gaze fixed on the road ahead as he tried to ignore the way his heart was pounding. She was so relaxed around him, clearly not realising how coquettish some of her actions appeared.

He didn't like the mischievous grin that spread over her face, a clear sign she was about to lead him down a dangerous path. "Why not? Are you keeping secrets from me, Preston?"

Only one. And that secret could ruin everything.

"Of course not," he lied. "I have no secrets. You could call me an open book."

"I do not know if I agree with that."

Her confession surprised him, that she thought he was hiding anything from her. Other than his one huge secret, he really was honest most of the time. "What makes you say that? You could ask me anything and I would answer."

Dark eyebrows arched over eyes glittering with mirth, her expression teasing. "Anything?"

"Bad choice of words." A reluctant smile tugged at the corners of his lips. "I obviously can't answer certain things." He was taunting her now, and he knew it, but she had this effect on him. "Take care not to offend my innocent sensibilities, please."

Amelia's burst of laughter was infectious, and it was impossible to keep his own inside. He loved these moments with her. Their easy banter and gentle teasing. He loved them, and he loathed them. Because he knew they would not be his forever. They were nothing but stolen moments, and they would all end, and his world would be all the darker for it.

Chapter Six

A few days later, the glittering ballroom of Lady Chisworth's townhouse was a world away from the intimacy of the carriage. The air hummed with the notes of a quadrille, the scent of roses, and overly perfumed bodies mingling with the excited chatter of the *ton*.

Amelia adjusted her fan, the delicate silk doing little to quell the heat of the crowded room. She had not heard from Preston since their ride in the park, and she missed his company. Which was very strange, indeed. This fake courtship had allowed her to interact with him in a different way to before, and she found that she rather enjoyed their conversations and easy banter.

But it was fake. It had to be. Nothing but a means to an end. No matter how her heart beat a bit quicker when they were alone in dark gardens.

After long walks in the park and a few tiresome visits with her aunt, she was ready to refocus on her plan, on Pensington. She wanted the safety of a good match, a solid future, and she would not be tempted down a dangerous path.

As the music came to an end, and the couples dispersed to the edge of the dance floor, a warm voice cut through her thoughts.

"May I have this dance?"

She pulled up her fan, pretending to be overheated so she could hide her grin, as she curtsied before the Marquess of Pensington. It wasn't the first time they had danced, but it had been some time since he had last asked her to stand up with him.

Hopefully, it was because she had caught his interest and not simply him being polite and ensuring everyone was dancing. It wasn't as if she lacked willing partners. Had she wanted to, she could have filled her dance card quite quickly. One of the advantages of being a duke's daughter. Also, one of the disadvantages.

While fully aware that she was privileged, she also knew that the level of interest she received was not wholly because people enjoyed her company, but also often because they wished to be seen with a duke's daughter. It made finding genuine friends difficult. Few young ladies were at her level, and as such they either feared her censure or simpered when she was near—both equally frustrating. She wasn't a difficult person to please. She really wasn't.

Part of the reason she had told Preston she wanted to befriend Pensington's sister had nothing to do with the handsome marquess at all. She simply hoped that a marquess's sister might be someone who could be a friend. She had so few of those.

As Pensington led her out onto the dance floor, she smiled up at him. As a marquess, he was one of the most eligible bachelors of the Season, and she could feel the eyes of every other unmarried young lady following them.

If anyone was to catch the marquess's attention, surely it ought to be her? Preston liked to remind her the man had no intention of marrying anytime soon, but as a titled lord, he would need a wife eventually, and she was determined to be in the forefront of his mind when that time came. Ideally, not too long from now.

"Are you enjoying the Season?" the marquess asked as they followed the precise steps of the dance, his movements graceful and controlled. He watched her with an almost curious interest, and her cheeks heated slightly as she wondered what he might be thinking as his gaze met hers.

The man really was one of the most handsome men of the *ton*, with his nearly black hair and equally dark eyes, his features sharp and refined. There was an upward twist at the corners of his mouth that gave him something of a wicked look. And yet, his light touches during the dance didn't seem to send the same shivers through her that Preston's did.

"I am, thank you." She smiled, hoping it appeared genuine. "How is your sister? I believe this is her first Season?"

"She is well, thank you." He smiled wryly, a hint of weariness in his eyes. "Though I suspect she would rather have stayed home at Davenhall reading books. Balls and parties are not exactly her preferred form of entertainment."

"A good book is certainly to be appreciated," Amelia said carefully, not wanting to seem too eager to dismiss the need for intellectual pursuits. "But I must confess that personally, I prefer life in London to the countryside most of the time. I enjoy meeting other people outside my family."

"I enjoy London too," the marquess admitted, his eyes scanning the room as they danced. "Though I am also very fond of my family, and I enjoy my time when I visit my country estate where they live."

She liked that he cared about his family. It was rather endearing.

"Perhaps my family is simply too boring." She giggled, her tone light, but she hoped he saw her for more than just the silly girl that she often appeared to be. Constantly smiling. Constantly pleasing. Constantly trying to find her place in the world. "If they were not such boring old codgers, I might enjoy time at home more."

The marquess chuckled. "I would never speak ill of your family."

"You may not," she agreed with a grin, tilting her head in a way that seemed to work on most men, and she hoped it would work on him too. "But I am their kin and may say all the wicked things I wish."

The chuckle morphed into a laugh, a richer, more genuine sound, and she was rather proud of herself for accomplishing it. A quick sweep of the ballroom confirmed others had noticed the marquess's amusement as well, their eyes lingering on them with thinly veiled curiosity.

Her gaze briefly met Preston's where he stood by the open terrace doors, a dark figure leaning against the frame, and he winked, lifting his glass in a mock salute. The hint of a knowing smile played on his lips.

Something in her stomach lurched, a strange mixture of irritation and longing, a sensation she could not explain. Forcing her gaze back to her dancing partner, she tried to forget the unwelcome feeling.

It proved harder than expected, the image of Preston lingering in her mind, and as the dance ended, the strange impulse to seek him out frustrated and annoyed her.

I just want to gloat about my progress.

It sounded like a lie, even to her. She had no need to gloat. This was not a game. It was her future. Grabbing a glass of punch from the refreshment table, she took a large sip, the cloying sweetness doing little to calm the restlessness within her.

Why was she thinking about Preston? He was her brother's friend. And in a strange sort of way, her friend. He was definitely not someone she would consider an option for marriage. He was a rake, and she had no interest in rakes, reformed or otherwise.

Her brows drew together as the object of her thoughts came ambling towards her, his drink still in his hand, his movements casual and effortless. His annoyingly handsome face was relaxed, his green eyes sparkling with suppressed mirth as he smirked at her unhappy countenance. The fact that his mere presence could affect her so strongly was beyond irritating.

"What has you glowering so?" he asked, his voice low and intimate as he fell into step next to her, his shoulders brushing against hers as she walked towards the terrace doors. The heat of the contact sent shivers down her spine, a reaction she couldn't explain.

"Nothing," she muttered, unwilling to disclose her thoughts, especially to him. She certainly would not reveal how much he affected her.

"I thought you would be overjoyed after dancing with Pensington," he mused, his words laced with a hint of teasing. "He seemed to enjoy himself."

"It was a good dance." Stepping out on the terrace, she took a deep breath of the cool evening air, trying to ignore the way her body reacted to his presence. She needed to be away from the heat, the intensity of him.

Obviously not finished talking, Preston followed. "That's it? 'It was a good dance'?" He frowned, his eyes searching her face. "What is the matter with you? This isn't the Amelia I know."

Turning to face him, she crossed her arms over her chest. "Nothing is the matter, Preston. Has it ever occurred to you that perhaps I am not always smiling? Not always the pleasant Amelia that has a kind or amusing word for everyone? That sometimes even I get weary?"

"No one can be constantly cheerful. I have never expected you to." He shook his head slowly as he stared down at her, his eyes searching her face, lingering a moment too long on her lips.

Seemingly without thinking, he reached out and tucked an errant lock of hair behind her ear, his fingers brushing against her temple. The heat of his touch sent a jolt of awareness through her body that almost made her flinch.

"I only meant that you seemed happy a moment ago," he continued softly. "Now, you appear to be miserable. Which makes me wonder what happened. Have I done something wrong?"

Lifting her hand to rub at her temple where he had just touched her, she closed her eyes for a moment, trying to regain her composure, her heart pounding against her ribs. "I appear to have developed a migraine," she mumbled. "I think I should return home."

"If that is what you wish." He sighed. "I will find your chaperone."

With that, he disappeared inside, leaving her alone on the terrace. His tall form melted into the crowd, and she felt oddly abandoned, a strange emptiness filling the space where he had been.

What was this madness? Surely she wasn't attracted to Preston? She could not be. It was all wrong, utterly wrong. Preston was everything she did not want.

And everything she did want.

He had a title—even if not quite as high as her father probably wished—he was handsome, and he made her smile. He was a good man, of that she was certain. But he was also a rake. Everyone knew so. And she could not allow herself to fall for a rake. Not again. She would not allow it. The memories of her last encounter with one were still too raw, too humiliating, and she refused to make the same mistake twice, no matter how tempting Preston might be.

Chapter Seven

Amelia was avoiding him.

It had been a week since she had abruptly left the Chisworth ball, claiming a migraine. A week since their almost-argument on the terrace, leaving him with more questions than answers. Preston adjusted his stance on the dance floor, scanning the room for the woman who occupied most of his thoughts while he followed the steps of the quadrille.

He was attending yet another ball on behest of their agreement. He smiled down at the young woman he was dancing with. When Amelia had teased him about enjoying dancing, she had been correct. He did. So if she made him go to these balls to act like her lovesick beau, then he might as well dance.

Two dances for Amelia, the rest he was free to dance with whomever he so chose. Currently, it was Miss Angelique Grafton, the younger sister of James Grafton, Viscount

Gowthorpe. She was perhaps a little out of practice on the dance steps, but a pleasant enough conversational partner that he did not mind.

Amelia had been strangely distant with him since the ball the previous week. Not distant enough to entirely ruin the impression that he was courting her, but he could tell the difference. There had been no impromptu visits to his house. No private chats in the corner of a ballroom. She'd even declined when he'd sent a note asking if she wanted to go for a ride in Hyde Park. This avoidance was more painful than he wished to admit.

Something was definitely wrong. But what had changed? He could not understand what he might have done to upset her, and that frustrated him. So far, he'd done everything she had asked of him. Admittedly, somewhat grudgingly, but he felt justified in his reluctance. Why was she avoiding him?

A quick glance confirmed she was currently dancing with Pensington. Was it progressing better than he had realised? That could explain why she had not sought him out.

If her plan was working, he would soon live out his usefulness. He didn't know how he felt about that. No, that wasn't true. He knew exactly how he felt about it. He just didn't want to dwell on it.

The dance ended, and he brought his dance partner back to her brother, then left after a curt bow. He'd seen Amelia sneak out into the garden—exactly the thing he had told her not to do. So after grabbing a glass of punch, he walked over to the open back doors and followed.

Hopefully, she had not snuck out to meet Pensington for a tryst. The thought left a sour taste in his mouth, which he tried to wash away with a mouthful of the sweet punch.

The white of a dress disappeared around a row of rose bushes as he came outside, the scent of the flowers mixing with the dampness of the evening air. What was she thinking, walking away from the house and the lights? If anyone discovered her out here with a man, it would be quite the scandal.

He debated whether he should go back inside to ensure he was not the one caught with her, but immediately discarded the thought. He had to know she was safe. Having been out in most of these gardens in the past, he knew a lot of the areas where one could hide from view, and could probably save her if someone came too close, or she found herself in a dangerous situation.

Stepping off the terrace and out into the garden, the grass crunched under his feet as he followed the path Amelia had taken, the lit lanterns casting long, distorted shadows along the way. It took him a few minutes of searching, but he eventually found her pacing back and forth inside a gazebo overburdened by ivy and clinging roses.

Muttering under her breath, she did not see him at first, allowing him a moment to watch her undisturbed. His heart clenched at her beauty with a longing that was almost painful.

In the dusky evening, her dark brown hair appeared almost black while the skin by her neckline was almost translucent in the pale moonlight seeping through the gaps in the leafy gazebo. With her white ball gown, she looked like a ghostly spirit as she strode from one side to the other, over and over, as if she were desperate for an escape from this place.

Taking another sip of his drink, he cleared his throat. She jumped, her head turning to stare at him, her brown eyes wide with a mixture of surprise and something else he couldn't quite place.

"Preston!" She sighed, her shoulders slumping as she realised she'd been found. "You gave me a scare."

"Beg your pardon." He leaned a shoulder against one of the wooden posts creating the foundation of the gazebo. "Is something the matter?"

"No, not at all." Something in her tone belied her words, and he narrowed his eyes.

"Are you certain? I feel like you have been avoiding me lately."

"Have I?" she asked, her tone light, but she was obviously lying. "I had not realised."

Lifting the glass to his lips, he took another swig, his eyes never leaving her face. She was definitely acting odd. "Are your plans with Pensington proceeding so well that you no longer need my help?"

He hated the way the words felt so bitter as they passed his lips, but he couldn't help it.

She stared at him for a moment as if she didn't understand his meaning, then she nodded. "Oh, yes. It's…" With a groan, she threw her hands out in a moment of frustration. "No. He has danced with me a few times, but is showing no sign of anything beyond polite interest. I might as well be one of his friends as far as he's concerned."

Was it bad of him to feel relieved? Probably. He did not care. "I did warn you when you started this," he pointed out, and was rewarded by a glare. It almost made him grin.

"Thank you for the reminder." She rolled her eyes, her arms folding tightly over her chest, and he fought the urge to pull her close and kiss the frown away.

Feeling a little guilty for being so happy about her failure, he pushed away from the ivy-clad post and took a step towards her. "I'm sorry, Amelia. But you will find someone." He forced an encouraging smile, trying to hide the truth in his eyes; that he wished it could be him. "Who wouldn't want you?"

She scoffed. "Lord Pensington, apparently."

"In his defence, he does not want a wife at all." He watched as she shifted from one foot to the other, her arms still across her chest. "Are you cold?"

"No."

"Is this why you have been avoiding me?" Maybe he should have stopped pushing, but her obvious attempts at not being alone with him over the past week were bothering him more than they should.

"I have not been avoiding you," she muttered, but her eyes would not meet his. When he quirked a brow, she sighed, her shoulders slumping. "Maybe a little."

He shook his head. While he'd suspected as much, he could not understand why. "Because you no longer need me?"

"Maybe." She shrugged, still refusing to look at him, her body tense and closed off. "It is not as if you have missed my company. You have been constantly dancing and speaking to other young ladies."

"Amelia?" His chest tightened as he realised the truth of it, hope and dread warring inside him. It seemed impossible, but… "Are you jealous that I am dancing with others?"

"No!" That denial came far too fast and far too forcefully. She appeared to realise the same as she made a face. "I am not proud of it," she muttered. "It's not as if I want to be jealous."

Realising he was holding on to the glass too tightly, he forced himself to relax his grip. "I don't understand," he said quietly. "You have no romantic interest in me."

She finally lifted her head to stare at him, her brown eyes clouded with anger and frustration. "I certainly do not wish to!" she snapped. "You are all wrong. But attraction cares little about suitability. It matters not. I am sure it is fleeting and so I will not bother you with it."

He took another step towards her, noting that she did not move away. "You are correct. Attraction cares little for anything. We cannot choose who we are attracted to."

"Life would be a lot easier if we could." Her voice was disgruntled, as if she would have bent the universe to her will if only it were possible.

A dark chuckle escaped him. "I could not agree more. It can be damned inconvenient. I should know."

Another step brought him before her, their bodies so close that he could feel her warmth in the evening air. She craned her neck to meet his gaze, her breathing shallow. "Why? Who are you attracted to?"

You.

The word hung unspoken between them as they stared at each other in the faint moonlight.

He gave her a self-deprecating smile, his gaze lingering on her lips. "I think you know."

"But you find me a nuisance. Adrian's annoying little sister." She shook her head, a thin line appearing between her brows.

"A very charming nuisance."

His free hand came up to cup her cheek, and she instinctively tilted her head to rest against his palm. He wanted to kiss her so badly, but that would be a terrible idea. A path to ruin.

Her breath hitched as she stood still, waiting, near enough that he smelled the light flowery scent he associated with her. Near enough that he only had to lean down slightly if he wanted to feel her lips against his. The temptation was so strong that there might as well have been a string between them, pulling them closer. And it was a fight he was quickly losing.

But he'd said he would never kiss her. That he would never jeopardise her honour. Forcing himself to drop his hand and step back was one of the hardest things he'd ever done.

Amelia's eyes followed him as he took another step backwards. She smiled wryly, her lips curling in a way he knew all too well. "Can't be that attracted to me then."

Sod it!

He dropped the glass, and it thumped as it hit the grass, the sound loud in the quiet garden, and he closed the distance between them again, pressing his mouth to hers in a searing kiss with more passion than finesse.

Amelia's hands came up to thread her fingers through the hair at the back of his head, holding him close. Embracing her, he pulled her closer, angling his head to deepen the kiss, his tongue stealing across her lips to taste her.

Kissing her was everything he had imagined and more. The way her warm body melted against his, the soft sighs as he teased her tongue with his own, the way his heart felt like it would burst with a love he couldn't express. This was a terrible idea. Because he never wanted to let her go. Never wanted to kiss another woman again. *Bloody hell.*

Pulling back, he rested his forehead against hers, their breaths mingling in the night air. She drew a shuddering breath. Then another. Her fingers disentangled from his hair, and her hands slid down to his chest, pressing against him... and he nearly lost his footing when she suddenly pushed him backwards, putting space between them.

"No!" she cried, her voice rising. "No, no, no! This is all wrong! *You're* all wrong!"

He stared at her, not entirely sure how to react. His brain still too preoccupied with the memories of their kiss. "What?"

She pointed an accusatory index finger in his direction. "You're a rake."

Frowning, he ran a hand through his hair, his mind spinning. "Yes," he admitted. "But that is not—"

"I have vowed never to fall for a rake again. They cannot be trusted. Never again!"

Before he could react, before he could say all the things that had been building inside him, she pushed past him and disappeared into the darker part of the garden. He stared after her.

Again?

The word echoed in his mind as he stared after her retreating form. Someone had hurt her, had made her fear rakes so completely that she would run from this connection between them. And suddenly, his reputation as a rake had never felt more like a curse.

Chapter Eight

Amelia cursed herself as she came to a stop in a corner of the garden, hidden behind some trees. It was darker in this part, the garden walls obstructing the moonlight filtering between the branches, and no lanterns had been placed this far out.

What had she done? She groaned. She had allowed Preston to kiss her. Preston! And it had been glorious. That might be the worst part. This was all wrong. It wasn't Preston that should kiss her, and she certainly should not be enjoying it. She could not allow herself to fall for a rake again.

Without thought, her hand came up to touch her mouth with hesitant fingers. The silk of her gloves was cool against her lips, but the memory of Preston's kiss was anything but cold. *Blast!*

"Amelia?" His voice cut through her annoyance and she automatically took a step towards it before remembering herself and backing further into her corner.

She didn't want to see him. It was mortifying to think how easily she had melted into his embrace. How her fingers had buried in his hair. What must he think of her?

"Please," he continued, and she saw his dark form coming from behind a row of bushes, the moonlight streaking his dark hair with silver. "Can we talk about this?"

She didn't want to talk. If she was absolutely honest, she wanted to keep kissing him, and that just wouldn't do. Preston was not who she wanted. *Pensington. I want Pensington.* The marquess, however, obviously had no interest in her. But she could not kiss Preston. He was her brother's friend. He was a rake. *He was almost everything she wanted.* With another quiet expletive, she backed another step, and a loud crack reverberated through the evening air as she stepped on a twig.

Preston's head snapped in her direction, the angles of his face in sharp relief in the faint moonlight. "Amelia?"

Frozen on the spot, she didn't dare to move. Barely dared to breathe. He was looking in her direction, his eyes narrowing as if trying to see past the darkness. Her insides lurched as he walked towards her, coming in underneath the tree branches. Standing still, he appeared to be searching the area for a sign of her.

"I can see your dress," he said after another moment. "I won't stay if you truly do not wish to speak to me, but I am hoping you will."

She sighed. Why had she chosen a white dress? Next time, she would wear something dark and muted. Just in case she wanted to hide.

"No," she muttered. "It's fine. It was childish to run away from you."

"You had every reason to. I should never have kissed you." He shifted from one foot to the other as his hand came up to rake through his hair. "I'm so sorry, Amelia... That was badly done of me. And highly improper."

He couldn't see her wry smile, so she let out a small scoff. She had basically taunted him to do it. Finding out he was attracted to her had been exhilarating. She had been berating herself for days after realising she was jealous about the attention he was giving other young ladies.

To discover he didn't only see her as Adrian's annoying little sister had been... A revelation. And she had wanted him to kiss her. So foolish. She should know better.

"No need to apologise," she said. "We were both caught up in the moment. It's easy to do foolish things under the cover of darkness."

"But I do need to apologise." He breached the distance between them and took her hand in his. Bringing it to his face, he placed a soft kiss on her knuckles. "I am the more experienced one here. I should know better."

The simple touch sent a warm shiver along her arm, and she snatched her hand back. His arm fell to his side, perhaps thinking she was rejecting his touch. Deciding it was safer if he believed that, she did not deprive him of the notion.

"Are you implying I'm too young and naïve to know what I want?" she said, her tone suitably icy.

"No, I—" He fell silent before letting out a warm chuckle. "Well, I suppose I am."

"Trust that I would not allow anyone to kiss me unless I wanted them to." She crossed her arms over her chest. "This is my second Season. I am not unaware of these things."

"Apparently."

Was that amusement in his voice? She scowled. "Are you laughing at me?"

"No." There was definitely a hint of laughter in his voice. She did not appreciate it one bit. "Amelia, I'm fully aware that you are not naïve, and I never intended to imply that you were. However," he added before she could interject. "As you like to point out—I am a rake. By definition, I should know better than to kiss a young, unmarried lady."

"Isn't kissing young ladies exactly what rakes do?" she muttered.

"Only disreputable ones." He lifted a shoulder in a shrug. "I will not lie and say I have not seduced enough women, but never one who did not wish to be, and certainly never someone who would be ruined if it was ever discovered. And I haven't—"

He stopped himself from finishing the sentence, and she wondered what he had been about to say. "You haven't what?"

"It doesn't matter. All I'm saying is that kissing you was a mistake, and for that, I am sorry. I never want to risk your reputation."

It always irked her when men would not tell her the whole story. As if her feminine sensibilities could not handle the truth. Her brothers and father were always trying to shield her, and while she knew it was out of love, it did not frustrate her any less.

Annoyed, she pushed past Preston, only to stop a few steps away and turn around. He was little more than a dark shadow below the trees, but that might be for the better. She didn't need to see his frustratingly handsome face.

"It is rather offending when you appear to believe I can not make my own choices. I allowed you to kiss me. The mistake is on both of us."

"Fine. I'm happy to share the blame." There was a moment's silence. "Amelia? What did you mean when you said 'never again' before?"

She groaned. "So you heard that."

A brief chuckle. "It was difficult not to."

"I'm sorry for my outburst." With a sigh, she leaned against the trunk of one of the larger trees. "If it helps, I was more angry with myself than with you. I have vowed never to look at another rake. And yet, here we are."

He watched her quietly for a moment. "Want to tell me about it?"

"Not particularly." She averted her face. It was too dark for him to see her properly, but she still couldn't bear to face him. It was such an embarrassing story. She had been such a fool.

The grass crunched under his shoes as he came up to her, his shadow appearing in the corner of her vision. His hand came up to tuck a finger under her chin, gently tilting her head back to face him. Moonlight filtered through the leaves above them where they stood, allowing her to make out some of his features as he stared down at her. Something in her abdomen did an awkward somersault.

"Whatever happened," he said quietly. "I hope you know I would never dishonour you. While I may have kissed you in a moment of weakness, I will never take advantage of you."

"I know that. While you are a rake, you're a good man." She made a wry face. "But I should know better than to kiss a man like you. There is no future with a rake, and I don't want to risk my reputation again."

"There is that word again." There was a hard edge to his words as he asked, "Who hurt you?"

"It's in the past. Let's not speak of it. I was young and foolish."

"Adrian has never mentioned anything of the sort," he said thoughtfully.

"For my protection, or I'm sure he would have." She wondered if he was aware that he was still touching her. His hand had dropped to her shoulder, where it rested gently against her skin, his thumb caressing a path above her clavicle. He wasn't wearing gloves, and the feeling of the pad of his thumb against her bare skin was oddly distracting, sending a shiver down her spine.

"He had a falling out with Lord Fulmer a few years ago." His eyebrows drew together as he watched her face for any signs of confirmation. "Fulmer is a bounder. Did he try anything with you?"

"I..." Maybe if he stopped touching her, she could gather her thoughts. But she also didn't want him to stop. "He spent a few weeks at our estate during the summer when I was sixteen. As I'm sure you know, he can be charming when he wants to, and I was taken with him. When Adrian wasn't looking, he promised me the world. Confessed his love. We would have escaped to Gretna Green together."

"Adrian found out?" Preston's hand on her shoulder flexed slightly, but he didn't move away.

"Yes. The night before we would have left." She sighed, the bitter memory still painful. Not because she had loved Fulmer. It had been an infatuation at best—she knew that now—but because she had been such a fool to believe his pretty lies. "During their argument, he admitted that he only cared for my dowry. Without it, he was not interested in anything beyond seducing me."

Preston let out a soft curse. "I can see why Adrian has not spoken to him since. It's a wonder he still has his teeth."

A little giggle escaped her. "Not for lack of trying." Sobering, she shrugged. "My family could have brought him down by telling everyone what he had tried to do, but they decided against it to save my reputation."

They fell into silence, but he still didn't remove his hand from her shoulder. "So this is why you are so against rakes."

It wasn't a question. She nodded anyway. "I have no interest in being nothing but another conquest for any man."

Another moment of silence. His hand had stilled, as if his mind was too preoccupied to keep the body moving. "Do you think so ill of me that you believe I would ever seduce you, only to leave you?"

She couldn't quite place the tone of his voice, but he sounded... wounded? "You... You are a rake," she pointed out. "It is always safer to stay away from one. Preferably six feet or more."

"This is nowhere near six feet." He shifted on his feet, moving slightly closer, and her heart skipped a beat. "I would like to think it's because you know I'm an honourable man."

"Is there such a thing as an honourable rake?" Her voice was more breathless than she'd have liked.

He chuckled darkly. "I suppose that depends on your definition."

"Would an honourable man have kissed me?" She was baiting him, and she knew it. But she enjoyed their light banter. Probably a little too much.

"No," he admitted. "But even honourable men can fail in the face of great temptation."

Her gaze flew to his eyes. They glittered darkly in the moonlight. Her breath hitched. "Temptation can definitely be difficult to resist." Her voice was little more than a whisper as he placed a hand on the tree trunk next to her head and leaned a little closer. Their breaths mingled.

"Almost impossible," he murmured, his eyes searching hers for an answer she wasn't sure she ought to give him. But oh, how she wanted him to kiss her again, to lose herself in his arms.

"I don't think anyone could blame an honourable man—or lady—for a moment of weakness," she whispered.

The hand on her shoulder came up to cup her face. His fingers were warm against her skin as he stared down at her, his thumb tracing a path across her jaw, sending shivers through her body.

"I think we both know society would blame them." The corners of his mouth twitched. "But perhaps no one needs to know of this... moment of weakness."

"No one."

His lips brushed against hers, and she almost forgot to breathe. Their previous kiss had been swift and passionate, and over too quickly. This time he took his time as his mouth came back to hers, teasing and nibbling, making her long for more before his tongue finally stole across her lips to deepen the kiss. Every stroke sent an arrow of excitement through her, hot desire growing and pooling low in her abdomen.

Trailing kisses along her jaw, he nipped at her earlobe before placing warm kisses on her neck. Her arms slid around his neck, her fingers threading through his dark hair. She had been kissed before, but even the skill of a rake like Fulmer was nothing compared to how Preston's simple, teasing touches sent warm anticipation coursing through her. This was so different—dangerous not because it might ruin her, but because it might make her forget why she needed to be cautious at all.

A teasing nibble below her ear sent a pleasurable shiver down her spine, and all thoughts of other men dispersed. There was only Preston and his hands and mouth.

"You taste amazing," he whispered against her skin. "I could kiss you for hours."

His mouth returned to hers as if to prove his words, capturing her lips in a searing kiss. She pressed against him, wanting more, wanting to feel him, and his hands drifted to her waist to pull her close. Even through the layers of their clothing, she could feel the evidence of his desire pressing against her abdomen. Slanting his mouth across hers, Preston deepened the kiss further, and she moaned against him. Their simple kiss had turned into something else, a fire raging between them, a longing she could no longer ignore.

As if he had the same thought, Preston pulled back, his breathing uneven. "This may not have been our best idea," he mumbled, his hand hovering over her cheek before he finally dropped it.

"Maybe not," she allowed, even as her body ached for more.

"But I cannot bring myself to regret it." His voice was low and husky as he looked down at her, his gaze lingering on her lips.

"Me neither."

They stared at each other through the dusk. Preston bowed his head, moving his other hand to rest against the tree trunk next to her, effectively trapping her between him and the tree. "Amelia, I—"

The sound of voices drifting close interrupted whatever he had been about to say, and he stepped away from her, putting space between them. "We should return inside before anyone notices we are gone," he whispered. "You go first, and I will follow in a few minutes."

She nodded, and after a quick look to make sure no one was near enough to see her, she exited the small gathering of trees and walked back to the ballroom, her heart still beating a frantic rhythm. Her lips still tingled with the memory of their kiss, distracting her enough to not notice where she was going until she collided with a wide chest on the terrace.

"Lady Amelia?" Lord Pensington was staring down at her, his eyes wide in surprise. "Are you all right?"

"Yes. Oh, yes. My apologies. I fear I was lost in thought." She flashed him one of her most charming smiles.

His gaze lingered on her lips for a moment, and she was suddenly struck by the fear that someone might be able to tell that she'd just been thoroughly kissed. Was that a thing? She wasn't sure. When he threw a glance towards the dark garden where she'd come from, her stomach dropped. Maybe it was possible. Would he tell anyone? Her reputation would be ruined.

"I… I went for a walk to clear my head," she said, the words sounding desperate even to her.

The marquess smiled gently. And was that a spark of amusement in his dark eyes? He cleared his throat. "Lady Amelia, would you like to keep me company on the terrace for a little while?"

It was her turn to stare. Was he interested in her, after all? "Oh. I would love to."

He leaned a little closer and her heart nearly stopped for a moment, but he only whispered in her ear, "May I suggest that you rearrange your hairdo? It's slightly askew."

She blinked, and her cheeks flushed hot with embarrassment. When he straightened, there was no mistaking the amusement lingering on his face. It was evident in the mischievous glitter in his eyes and the slight turn of his lips. She should be grateful that he was helping her hide the evidence of what she had done out in the garden, but right then, she was mortified more than anything else. How had she allowed herself to get so close to ruin?

"Thank you," she mumbled as her hands flew up to her hair, trying to fix the mess she had created. *That Preston had created.*

"It's no problem." The marquess smiled down at her, his gaze lingering on her a moment too long, his voice warm with amusement. "We've all needed a moment after a... stroll in the gardens late at night."

He winked. Amelia groaned inwardly. Her grand plans for this Season were not going very well. Not very well at all.

Chapter Nine

Kissing Amelia might be the worst, and simultaneously the best, thing Preston had ever done. He could not stop thinking about it. Could not stop remembering the feel of her soft lips against his. Her body in his arms. Finding out she was attracted to him had been his undoing. How could he possibly resist her now?

But where did that leave them? They needed to talk. Which was why he found himself at the residence of the Duke of Hoyton the following morning for social calls. He didn't relish the idea of calling on Amelia so publicly, but he wanted to see her—no, he *needed* to see her. And if he was considering throwing his hat in the ring, he might as well let it be known now.

The ageing butler had taken his calling card, as well as that of another young man who had arrived a mere moment after Preston, and disappeared to inform the family of their arrival.

Nodding to his fellow man and potential rival, he groaned as he saw Richmond coming down the grand staircase leading from the upper floor to the entrance hall. *Brilliant.*

"Leighton!" Richmond bowed his head in greeting as he caught sight of him. A brief nod towards the other man. "Greyson."

"Lord Richmond." The young man bowed while Leighton only nodded his head, wary of what the future duke would make of his presence.

The butler reappeared. "Lord Leighton. Mr Greyson. You may enter the drawing room now."

Richmond's dark brows furrowed as he watched the younger man hurry down the hallway before turning his pale blue eyes to Preston. "What are you doing here?"

Steeling himself, Preston forced a pleasant smile on his face. "I've come to call on your sister."

"The hell you have."

"I have."

Richmond's frown deepened, and he took a step closer. They were of equal height, and while Preston doubted the other man was much of a pugilist, he didn't particularly want to find out. Especially in Richmond's home.

"I thought I made myself clear," Richmond practically growled. "You are to stay away from Amelia."

"I think we should allow her to make that decision." He should probably be grateful it was Richmond who'd seen him and not Adrian. His friend would have had no compunction about throwing him out on his arse, probably after a solid right hook. Richmond, fortunately, was more tempered. Still, it was obvious the other man did not appreciate being contradicted.

"We want someone better for Amelia," he said coldly, his blue eyes like ice. "I won't have you ruin her chances of a good match."

Preston scoffed, annoyed at the way the other man looked down on him, and a small part of him wondered if he would ever be considered good enough for her. "I doubt my mere presence today will make anyone change their mind about whether to court her or not."

"I don't want you anywhere near her."

"Fortunately, you do not get to decide," Preston said, his voice tight. "I may only be a viscount, but my family is one of the oldest in the country. It's not a terrible match!"

Richmond's frown relaxed for a moment as his eyes widened slightly. "What? I do not care about your title. Amelia could marry a pauper for all I care, as long as she'd be happy. Everyone knows you're a rake. She is not some conquest for you to win."

All of his indignant anger seeped out of him. He'd been so angry about the perceived slight to his lower title, but really Richmond doubted his sincerity based on, in fairness, completely valid concerns, and he had completely misjudged the man. He *did* have a reputation as a rake.

With a sigh, he ran a hand through his hair. "Richmond, I understand your apprehension. Truly. But my intentions regarding your sister are honourable. I would never dream of risking her reputation."

A brief memory of Amelia pressed against him as he kissed her the previous night flashed before his eyes, but he pushed it away. His intentions were *largely* honourable. Richmond didn't need to know of his moment of weakness.

"I don't know." Richmond crossed his arms over his chest. "My sister means a lot to me and I will not see her hurt in any way."

"I appreciate your concern for your sister's happiness. I do." *If only you weren't so bloody stubborn about it.* "But I swear to you, I am only wanting the chance to court her. You must know that while I'm known as a rake, I've also never been one to give attention to innocents. I have never ruined anyone, and I have no intention of starting now."

Richmond huffed, but stepped out of the way, his gaze lingering on him a moment longer. "Fine," he muttered. "But I'm watching you."

"Wouldn't expect anything less." Preston sketched a quick bow before walking down the hallway to the drawing room. If he'd had a sister, he probably would have done the same thing.

The house was what one would expect of a duke's home; grand and opulent, showing off every ounce of their long and noble heritage, with paintings of ancestors on the walls, expensive furniture, and fancy wallpapers. The drawing room was no less impressive with its light blue walls and mahogany wainscoting, the scent of roses and beeswax polish thick in the air.

A pianoforte stood by a window, and a woman Preston recognised as the formerly snoozing chaperone Aunt Ruth played a song for a group of visitors, the melody of the melancholic piece drifting through the room.

Preston heard Amelia before he saw her. He would recognise that bubbling laughter anywhere. She stood further into the room beyond a set of settees and comfortable chairs, surrounded by a bevy of suitors. The number of bachelors in attendance shouldn't surprise him, but he'd forgotten just how popular she was.

Just because she hadn't found a husband didn't mean she didn't have plenty of options. As the daughter of a duke, she was an excellent match for anyone. Add her beauty and sparkling personality, and few men could resist the allure. Who wouldn't take the chance to court her? The sight of them all vying for her attention made his chest tight with an emotion he refused to name as jealousy.

Was he a fool to even consider trying?

Venturing further into the room, he saw when she noticed him as her eyes widened slightly. He'd never visited any young lady during the day before, so his presence was eliciting some murmurs among his fellow callers as well.

If he'd known quite how busy Amelia would be, he might have waited to see her at a more convenient time. But his mind had not wanted to think about things rationally. All he'd known from the moment he woke up was that he needed to see her again. The moment he'd kissed her, every objection—every reason he had for staying away from her—had vanished.

He wanted Amelia. Everything else be damned.

And as long as he could persuade her to accept his suit, he would make her his wife. He just needed to convince her he was a suitable match, after all. That he was more than a rake. He was a man who loved her and he would do anything to make her happy. If only she would let him.

Chapter Ten

Amelia's stomach did an awkward somersault as she caught sight of Preston among the visitors crowding the drawing room. What was he doing here? This wasn't his type of scene. Was he making a statement? She gingerly touched her lips as she remembered his feverish kisses the previous night. They tingled from the mere memory, and she'd be lying if she said she didn't want to experience that again.

But she needed to remain in control. Focus on her pursuit of the marquess. Preston was all wrong. How could she trust a rake to give up his rakish ways? She didn't think he would risk her reputation—she believed him when he swore he never would—but she still had never envisioned herself married to a rake.

Why would one so used to going from woman to woman suddenly be content with only one? It was difficult to fathom, and while she knew many women of the *ton* simply accepted the reality of their husbands having affairs as long as they were discreet, she did not think she was one who could be content in sharing her husband. He had to be fully hers or not at all, and that seemed unlikely for a rake.

Even if he was the most handsome man in attendance.

She pushed the thought away, even as she failed to make her gaze do the same. Dressed in a dove-grey tailcoat with matching breeches and black Hessian boots, Preston cut a dashing figure with his wide shoulders and narrow hips.

She'd always liked his dark hair; the way a comb could never quite tame it, and it always looked a little as if he'd just stepped in from the windswept moors of the Lake District. Which was, incidentally, where his estate was located. So she supposed it was only right. The fact that she knew such details about him, and had noticed them long before their kiss, was something she refused to examine too closely.

As he approached, she schooled her features into a mask of polite interest, not wanting him to notice her gawking. Nor anyone else, for that matter. A proper young lady did not gawk at a gentleman, especially not a notorious rake like Preston.

He stopped before her and the handful of admirers who were all vying for her attention. But she only had eyes for Preston. Which she shouldn't. He was not for her. Something she would do well to remind herself of. Continuously. No matter how good his kisses were.

"Lady Amelia," he said as he bowed his head in greeting, and even the rich cadence of his voice was enough for her pulse to quicken. This was ridiculous. She desired a safe and proper match, not this... this wicked man who made her heart flutter.

"Lord Leighton." She curtsied while praying her cheeks were not as flushed as they felt.

After a nod to her companions, he mumbled, "Gentlemen."

The group all returned the favour, and for once she was grateful for the stilted politeness of their peers. It allowed her a moment to breathe before his green eyes returned to hers.

Everything was all wrong lately. Preston wasn't the one who should make her feel like this, and yet he was, and he was the only one to. Even the handsome Marquess of Pensington did nothing to make her pulse quicken or her insides flutter, and that worried her. The marquess sounded good on paper, but in reality, she was forced to recognise that she had no romantic interest in him.

"Oh, bother!"

Five sets of eyes turned on her and she cursed inwardly. She had not intended to say that out loud. Pretending to cough, she hoped they'd believe she had something stuck in her throat. Or, at the very least, were polite enough not to question her.

"Is something the matter?" Preston's eyes glittered as she glared at him. Trust him not to allow her the graceful way out.

"Just a tickle in my throat," she replied with a forced smile, trying to maintain some level of composure.

"Oh." He mirrored her polite smile. "I could have sworn I heard you say something."

His eyes twinkled, and she wanted nothing more than to push him into the nearest wall. And possibly kiss him. No! Definitely not kiss him. No more kissing him.

One of her admirers, Mr Denton, cut in. "The air is quite dry. It's easy to get a scratchy throat."

Baron Edgerton puffed his barrel-sized chest. "I could never imply that the air in the duke's house is dry," he said pompously. Turning to her, his bushy eyebrows knotted, reminding her of two furry caterpillars huddling together for a secret sojourn. "My dear Lady Amelia, I do hope you are not coming down with a cold. Can I get you anything? Shall we get you another cup of tea?"

Unsure whether she wanted to roll her eyes or laugh, she shook her head. "No, thank you. I'm better already."

"I believe what the lady needs is a turn about the room," Preston said and offered her his arm.

She stared at it for a moment before putting her hand in the crook of his elbow, the warmth of his body a dangerous temptation. "That would be lovely, thank you."

As he led her away from the group of men, she tried not to look back at their baffled faces, nor at the smirk on Preston's lips.

"You are finding this far too amusing," she admonished, her voice a low whisper so as not to be overheard.

Turning his head to look down at her, his smirk dissolved into an amused grin, and her heart skipped a beat. "I cannot help enjoying disappointing your bevy of suitors. They might as well be a group of puppies swarming you in the hopes of their next treat."

She bit the inside of her cheek to keep from smiling at his comparison. "They are all good men."

"But they do not interest you." It wasn't even a question. She supposed she had told him enough times she had no interest in anyone but the marquess. But it still irked her that he knew her so well.

"No," she admitted. As they moved along the sides of the room, she nodded and smiled at those they passed, affording her a good excuse not to stare up at Preston.

"Has Pensington ever shown up?"

She scoffed. "You know he has not." Tilting her head, she gave him a quick, surreptitious glance, but his face was a polite mask as he looked out over the room. "What of you? Why are you here?"

Maybe she shouldn't ask, but she was curious. To her knowledge, Preston had never called on any young lady during visiting hours. So why was he here? An attempt at making their pretend-courtship appear more real?

He looked down, his eyes meeting hers, something unreadable in their depths. "After last night—"

"Last night was a mistake!" she hissed under her breath, trying to ensure no one could hear them. "I believe we both discussed how we cannot choose who we are attracted to. Our mistake was giving in to said att—"

"I am here to toss my hat in the ring." His words cut her short and her eyes widened.

"Pardon?" She must have misheard.

A smile tugged at the corner of his mouth. "I am planning to court you. The old-fashioned way. And not as a favour for you to capture the interest of another man, but because I want to."

Thoughts were swirling in her head, but none of them made sense. Court her? What was he thinking?

"I... What? Preston, you cannot!" She realised her grip on his arm had become rather strained, and she forced herself to loosen her fingers. "I expect nothing after yesterday. You must realise that?"

"I do," he said, his tone easy. "And you will find that I can. And I will."

"But why?"

He glanced out over the room before lowering his head slightly towards her, his voice a low whisper that sent shivers down her spine. "I believe that is a discussion for another time, with less of a potential audience."

She caught a whiff of his scent. Something woodsy and manly. And intrinsically *him*.

"But you're a rake." Not her finest retort, but her mind was struggling to keep up, too preoccupied remembering the feel of his lips on hers.

He shrugged. "Even rakes get married."

"Not to me."

"So you say, but I would like the chance to convince you otherwise." They had returned to her group of suitors, and with a bow, Preston left her side, apparently content that he had said his piece.

Staring after him as he left the drawing room, she pretended his words didn't make her insides flutter. Didn't make her want to know exactly how he intended to do that. And most of all, she pretended she wasn't terrified by how much she wanted him to succeed.

Chapter Eleven

Later that day, Preston sat at his desk sorting through some correspondence when there was some commotion outside the door to his combined library and study. Curious, he put the papers down and stood, but before he could move further than the other side of his desk, the door opened and his butler entered, his white brows drawn in what would have been annoyance in someone less accomplished in looking proper at all times.

"My lord." Giles cleared his throat. "Lady Amelia has come to call."

The butler barely had time to finish the sentence before Amelia burst through the door behind him. Preston had to work hard not to grin at the scene, even as his heart leapt at the sight of her. The wings of Giles's hawk-like nose flared. This was not something the strict butler would appreciate. An unmarried young lady should not be calling on a bachelor, and she most certainly should not be forcing herself into his study without waiting to be invited.

"Thank you, Giles." Preston nodded to the old man, who left with a barely perceptible huff and closed the door behind him.

"What are you playing at?" Amelia snapped as she stopped halfway into the room, one of her hands motioning in the air as if she was pointing to something more tangible than a declaration she had not appreciated.

Amused, he leaned his hips back against his desk and crossed his arms over his chest. "I thought we talked about how it's a bad idea for you to visit me on your own?"

Her eyes caught his, and her brows knotted. "I am not in the mood for teasing, Preston," she said, her voice laced with frustration. "What was that spectacle this morning? Coming to call on me? In front of everyone! Richmond even took me aside after and reminded me of what a rake you are and that I ought to be careful around you."

"It was exactly what I said it was." The calmer he remained, the more agitated she appeared to become. Unable to stay still, she paced the room, the skirt of her dress swishing with every step. But his next words stopped her short. "I wish to court you, Amelia."

"No." She shook her head, making the carefully arranged curls at her temples bounce.

"No? Just no? I don't even get a reason?"

"You know my objections."

"Ah yes." He stood and took a step towards her. "I am a rake and you have no interest in rakes."

"Exactly." She chewed on her lower lip as she watched him, and it did not escape his notice that she had not moved away as he came closer.

"That's rather narrow-minded, don't you think?" He was enjoying this far too much. It was an unusual sight to see Amelia's feathers ruffled. "Do you not believe people can change?"

She huffed. "A rake choosing to spend his life with one woman when he's used to chasing after plenty? I think not."

Lifting one shoulder in a shrug, Preston took another step towards her. "It happens. We all grow up and realise we must settle down eventually."

"Very romantic," she muttered, sarcasm practically dripping from the words.

He lifted an eyebrow, fighting the smile tugging at his lips. "Would you like me to be?"

She shifted from one foot to the other as her eyes avoided his. "N... No. It was just an observation." Finding her confidence again, her brown eyes narrowed at him. "And deciding to settle down is not the same as choosing to be faithful to your wife."

"That is true. I cannot argue with your logic." When she opened her mouth to say something else, he continued, "However, I would like the chance to prove you wrong. And you should know that when I marry, I will never stray from the marriage bed."

"You can't know that."

"I can. Because I am a man of my word." Taking the final steps separating them, he took her gloved hands in his and brought them to his lips for a soft kiss, his gaze searching hers. Her mouth dropped open as she stared up at him. "And if you were my wife, why would I ever want anyone else?"

Her eyes widened, and she pulled her hands out of his as if she'd been burned. Taking a step away, she shook her head slightly. "Preston, I... Why are you doing this?" Her voice was barely above a whisper.

Frustrated, he dragged his hand through his hair. He hadn't planned on confessing his feelings yet for fear of scaring her off, but she had pushed him into a corner. Admitting to attraction was a lot easier than pouring his heart out, and he struggled to find the right words to fully convey how he felt, how he'd changed.

Amelia bounced a fisted hand against her thigh as she watched him, waiting for an answer, and he realised she was wearing a ball gown. He frowned.

"Are you on your way somewhere?"

"I'm due at the coming-out-ball of Viscount Gowthorpe's sister and cousin. But I wanted to talk to you before I went. My aunt has gone ahead of me, and I will meet her there. I could not stop thinking about this morning and what you said. It makes no sense to me."

He grinned. "You've been thinking about me?"

She glared at him. "That is not what I said."

His grin widened. "It sort of is."

"You can be rather infuriating when you wish to be," she muttered.

"I can also be rather charming when I wish to be." He was rewarded by a twitch at the corner of her mouth.

"You must tell me why you are doing this." Her imploring tone erased his amusement. "You said you would tell me at a better time." She swept an arm out. "There is hardly a better time than this, as we are completely alone."

"Yes." He sighed. "We really should not be. You must stop visiting me like this. It would be quite the scandal if anyone found out. You're lucky my servants are loyal and won't gossip."

"Then don't barge into my home and tell me you plan to court me," she snapped, her temper getting the better of her. "And then refuse to tell me why."

He chuckled. "Pardon? Who barged into whose home?"

Her eyes narrowed. "Are you avoiding the question?"

"Maybe a little." Retreating, he leaned his hips against his desk again as she watched him from across the room. "I already told you I'm attracted to you."

"Attraction is no reason to marry," she countered. "Our mutual attraction is nothing but an inconvenience that we simply will have to deal with. You owe me nothing simply because we shared one kiss."

"I remember it as being decidedly more than one," he said darkly, making her cheeks darken slightly.

"Still," she pressed on. "I expect nothing from you, and the entire ordeal is probably better forgotten by both of us."

Putting his hands on either side of his hips on the desk behind him, he leaned forward slightly, his gaze not leaving hers. "See, that's the trouble," he drawled. "I cannot forget kissing you. Nor would I ever want to."

"I..." Amelia inhaled and touched her temple, trying to tuck the loose dark curls behind her ear but quickly giving up. "I will agree that our kisses were... pleasant. However, that does not—"

Preston stood, pushing away from the desk. "Pleasant?" He knew she was trying to downplay what had happened, but the word choice wounded his male pride. The kisses they had shared were definitely better than *pleasant*.

Amelia's cheeks had grown another shade darker and her hands fluttered aimlessly, as if she didn't quite know what to do with them. "Well... Yes, I mean—"

"If they were only pleasant, I must be out of touch," he muttered. Caught by a wicked spirit, he gave her a teasing grin. "Perhaps I must ask for a do-over. To prove myself."

"You are not amusing." She crossed her arms over her chest as she glared at him. "You know full well your kisses were more than adequate."

"More than adequate?" He let out a bark of laughter. "Is that meant to be a compliment? Please do not try to encourage me further, I am not certain my pride could take it."

"What do you want me to say?" she practically growled. "That they were the most amazing kisses ever?"

Crossing the room to stand in front of her, he lifted his hand to touch the bouncy curls she had played with earlier, his fingers trailing along the soft strands. "That'd be a start," he murmured. "Earth-shattering would be an excellent description."

A smile fluttered across her lips. "I hardly believe your pride needs further inflation."

His hand lowered to her chin, and his thumb grazed her bottom lip. "So you do not need a demonstration to ensure you have the right idea?"

She closed her eyes for a moment. "Preston," she whispered, and he almost kissed her then. "Do not toy with me."

He waited until her eyes fluttered open again to meet his gaze before he smiled slightly. "I would never toy with you. Tease you, yes. Always. But I would not toy with your emotions. I meant what I said earlier, Amelia. I intend to court you. It is my hope that I can convince you to be my wife."

"But why?" Her question was barely more than a breath against his hand. The moment stretched between them, and he knew once he spoke these words, there would be no taking them back. But he was tired of hiding, tired of pretending his feelings were anything less than what they were.

"Because I love you."

They stared at each other as the declaration hung heavy between them. Then Amelia suddenly turned on her heel and dashed out of the room. Preston stared after her. Not quite the reaction he had hoped for. He sighed. Amelia never acted the way one might expect, but he really was getting rather tired of her running away from him.

Chapter Twelve

Maybe she ought to stop running away from Preston whenever she didn't want to continue a conversation. Amelia considered this possibility as she forced a pleasant smile while dancing with the Marquess of Pensington. Her handsome dance partner was charming, but she managed little more than a few nods and smiles as Preston's words preoccupied her mind, and her body still tingled from his touch.

Just hours ago, his fingers traced her lips, and now here she was, dancing with the man she'd thought she wanted, feeling nothing but polite interest. Everything was upside down.

'Because I love you.'

Nonsense! Preston didn't love her. He couldn't love her. She frowned. Could he? They had only shared a few kisses. He'd admitted to being attracted to her, but love? If he had harboured feelings for her, he had certainly hid it well. She had never considered the possibility that he thought of her as anything other than his friend's annoying little sister. An annoying little sister he was attracted to. Could he have been hiding more than his attraction? Had she truly been so blind?

And those kisses. Her cheeks burned. No, she would do well not to think about those, lest they distract her from her true goal. A safe match. Someone who couldn't possibly break her heart, and that was most definitely not a rake!

"Lady Amelia?" Lord Pensington's soft question brought her back to the present, and she gave him an apologetic smile. She was lucky to know the steps of the dance so well she could do it in her sleep, or she might have stepped on his toes by now.

"My apologies, Lord Pensington. I fear I was concentrating too much on my dancing," she lied.

The shadow of a smile crossed his lips as he looked down at her, and she couldn't help but wonder if he was recalling meeting her after she had obviously been thoroughly kissed by someone. She rather hoped not. The marquess was known as an honourable man, and she did not want him to think she was open to such behaviour, which, of course she absolutely was, but only with the wrong man.

"Not to worry," he said, his voice low and almost intimate. "I have to focus at times myself. It is far too easy to let your mind wander."

He glanced at the crowd with a hint of something almost like longing, and she wondered if he was also thinking of someone he wasn't supposed to.

Deciding to change the subject, she nodded towards a group of men hovering around two young ladies. "It would appear your friend Viscount Gowthorpe's sister is doing well at her coming-out-ball."

The marquess's face clouded as he followed the direction of her nod, his gaze lingering particularly on Miss Grafton before he spoke. "Yes," he muttered. "If I'm honest, I don't know whether Gowthorpe is pleased for her or worried about having to fight any undesirable suitors off with a stick."

Amelia laughed quietly, and unable to stop herself, she gave him a mischievous smile. "It must be quite difficult to be on the other side of the experience for him."

It took a moment before he caught her meaning, and for a moment she wondered if she had overstepped, but then he laughed. "True. He should appreciate the plight of fathers and brothers everywhere more." Looking away from Miss Grafton with what appeared to be great effort, he added so quietly she was fairly certain she wasn't meant to hear it, "Maybe we both should."

While the comment definitely piqued her interest, and she couldn't help but notice how his eyes kept straying back to the other young woman, she decided they didn't know each other well enough to pry, so she remained silent. Once the dance finished, the marquess led her off the floor, and after a polite bow, he disappeared to find his friend.

Noting that Aunt Ruth was busy chatting to some other matrons, Amelia fetched herself a glass of punch and slipped out onto the terrace before any of her suitors could find her. With new prey for them to admire, there seemed to be a few less than usual. Something she did not mind as it could get quite tiring having a group of men hover around her, vying for her attention. Especially knowing that they cared little for her as a person, and cared more for her family connections and dowry.

The warm spring evening made the terrace a welcome respite, with several others also seeking to cool down from the warm ballroom. A few couples walked along the lit paths in the garden below, but Amelia felt content to remain on the terrace tonight. Moonlit gardens had not been good for her composure lately, so she was probably better off staying away.

Leaning her hip against the terrace railing, she took a sip of her punch and closed her eyes. A light breeze played with the loose curls at her temples, lulling her into a moment of peace.

"Amelia."

She groaned inwardly, her body instantly reacting and her pulse quickening. Opening her eyes, she looked at Preston as he came to stand next to her at the railing, hating how attracted she was to him. He was handsome in his evening attire. Black tailcoat and trousers, matched with a grey waistcoat, white shirt and cravat. His dark hair looked a little more unkempt than usual, as if he'd dragged his hand through it one time too many, and she had to fight the urge to reach out and smooth the unruly strands.

Leaning his back against the railing, he crossed his arms over his chest as he stared down at her. "You ran away from me," he said. "Again."

She made a face. "I'm sorry."

He sighed, and after a quick glance to make sure no one was near enough to hear them, he leaned a little closer. "Am I to believe you did not appreciate my declaration?"

"More... I didn't expect it."

A dark brow rose at her reply. "And that warranted your swift exit?"

"I wasn't sure how to handle the situation."

"So leaving was the obvious option?"

"Apparently."

He chuckled. A pleasant sound that trickled over her like warm honey. He shook his head. "What am I to do with you, Amelia?"

Feeling unusually brave—possibly because they were around others—she met his eyes. "What would you like to do with me?"

His mouth opened as he stared at her, and for a moment she saw his arms relax before he tightened them across his chest again. When his gaze dropped to her mouth, she automatically wet her lips with her tongue, her body reacting before she could even think. His eyes came back to hers, the look in them darker than usual.

"Amelia," he said quietly. "I think you know exactly what I want to do with you."

A spear of excitement shot straight down her spine and set off a fluttering of tiny butterflies in her abdomen. This was a dangerous game they were playing.

"Tell me," she whispered, her heart pounding so hard she was sure he must be able to hear it. What was she doing, encouraging him like this? And yet she didn't want to stop.

Preston watched her quietly for a moment, making the fluttering inside her intensify until she thought she might burst. Finally, he leaned closer, his breath fanning her temple, and she almost stopped breathing.

"I want to kiss you so thoroughly that you forget your own name," he murmured, causing gooseflesh to spread across her skin as his lips grazed the shell of her ear. "And then I want to slowly strip you of every piece of clothing and worship your body. Show you exactly how I feel about you. I—"

"What the hell?"

Preston straightened and Amelia pulled back as they both turned to find her brother standing a few feet away, staring at them. Her stomach dropped as she saw his brown eyes—so alike her own—burning with indignant anger.

The world seemed to tilt beneath her feet as reality crashed back in. She'd been so caught up in Preston, in the heat building between them, that she'd forgotten where they were, forgotten everything but him. Now shame and fear warred with lingering desire, making her head spin.

"Adrian," she said, forcing a light tone, desperately trying to appear calm when she was anything but. "It's good to see you again. When did you return to London?"

Her brother ignored her, his attention focused on Preston, the fury in his eyes terrifying. "Leighton? What the hell are you doing? When Richmond said you were hanging around Amelia, I didn't believe him. Or at the most, I thought you might simply be courteous by keeping her company in my absence. Then I see you out here like this?"

A few other guests cast glances in their direction, so she walked up to her brother and took his hand, trying to pull him away. "Welcome home, brother," she said pointedly. "Let's not make a scene in public."

He made a sound low in his throat that wasn't entirely unlike a growl, but nodded, his jaw tight with anger. "Fine," he said tersely. Then, with another glare in Preston's direction, he added, "This discussion is not finished."

"I suspected as much," Preston muttered, earning him another glare.

"Gowthorpe's library," Adrian said, his gaze fixed on his friend. "Ten minutes."

Preston nodded, and she gave him an apologetic smile over her shoulder as her brother escorted her back into the ballroom. She groaned inwardly. She was in so much trouble. Could Adrian have chosen a worse moment to appear? Actually, he probably could have. If he'd have seen them the other night...

Kissing. She didn't want to consider what his reaction might have been to that.

Glancing up at her brother's tense profile, she felt a mixture of guilt and defiance. She hadn't planned to be attracted to Preston—had, in fact, been determined to be the opposite—but she couldn't deny how her body still tingled from his touch, or the way her heart raced when near him. Not even Adrian's anger seemed to douse the fire burning inside her.

What was Adrian planning to tell Preston in the library? Or, perhaps more importantly, what was Preston going to tell her brother?

Chapter Thirteen

It was not with a little trepidation that Preston entered Gowthorpe's library a short while later. He wasn't sure what he had hoped to accomplish by following Amelia to the ball, but he knew this definitely wasn't it. What a bloody mess!

Adrian was his best friend, and he always enjoyed his company, but for possibly the first time in his life, he wished the man had not shown up. Maybe he should be grateful they had not been kissing. Finding him leaning close to Amelia whispering in her ear wasn't much better, though. Such familiarity was definitely not proper.

The Warble siblings were arguing when he entered the room, but stopped when they heard the soft click of the door closing behind him. As they turned towards him, it struck him how similar they were in both looks and personality.

They had the same dark brown hair and brown eyes, and they both enjoyed a good laugh. He supposed it was no wonder he enjoyed the company of both. Though Amelia's in a far different way to her brother's.

Adrian crossed his arms over his chest as he stared at Preston, his brow furrowed. "Care to explain what's going on?" he asked, his voice hard.

"Not particularly," Preston admitted honestly, earning him a glare. His friend did not appreciate his humour today.

"Because it looked to me like you were trying to seduce my sister." One of Adrian's arms flung out to point toward Amelia. "My sister, Leighton! You usually steer clear of innocent, unmarried women for the same reasons I do, so to think you would so easily dishonour my sister is beyond belief!"

"Then don't believe it," Preston muttered, then as Adrian's face darkened and he took a step towards him, he quickly added, "Because I never would, damn it! I don't know what Richmond told you, but I made it clear to him that my intentions towards Amelia are honourable."

"That's not what it looked like."

Considering what he had been whispering in Amelia's ear, Preston wasn't surprised. Honourable might be pushing it. He wanted to do many wicked things with her. A quick glance confirmed that she still hovered behind her brother. Her eyes narrowed, as she watched their argument. He suspected she did not enjoy being spoken about as if she wasn't there.

"I wish to court her," he said. "I've been asking her permission to do so." That wasn't too far from the truth.

"Court her?" Adrian let out a surprised bark of laughter. "But she's my sister!"

"I'm aware of that. Despite that one flaw of character—" He paused for a moment as Amelia snorted with laughter, then continued, "I'm rather fond of her."

"You are not nearly as amusing as you think you are," Adrian growled. "But fine. You wish to court her. You cannot."

Preston straightened as he met his friend's icy stare. "I am rather tired of being told who I can and cannot court. The only one whose opinion I care about in this regard is Amelia's."

"You're a rake!" Adrian spat.

"So are you! The day you wish to court a lady, I hope her family is less judgemental about your past than you are about mine."

They stared at each other for several breaths, and Preston couldn't help but wonder if his friend would punch him.

Adrian groaned. "I see your point," he said, and Preston breathed a sigh of relief. "But I struggle to see you with Amelia. She's my sister, damn it, and I don't want her with a rake."

"I think she should be allowed to choose for herself." He could only hope she would choose him.

His heart hammered in his chest as Adrian turned to his sister. She looked like a deer caught in the hunter's aim. "Amelia? Do you want Leighton to be allowed to court you?"

"I... We..." Her gaze flicked between her brother and Preston and back again.

Her words stalled, and his stomach plummeted. Maybe attraction was the only thing she felt for him. The rake was good for no more than a few kisses, after all. The pain of that realisation was sharper than he'd expected, cutting straight through him.

"Never mind," he forced out, his voice rough with pain and rejection. "I suppose that is the answer I needed."

Without waiting, he turned around and exited the library, leaving the two siblings behind. He wasn't sure what he'd been expecting. Had it not been enough of a hint when Amelia kept running away from him whenever he confessed to his feelings? Bloody hell, what a fool he'd been.

Not wanting to rejoin the other guests in the ballroom, he walked in the opposite direction and was about to turn a corner when Amelia's voice stopped him in his tracks.

"Preston!"

He closed his eyes. He wasn't sure he wanted to see her right now. Didn't want to hear her excuses for why she didn't want him. Didn't want her pity. Her steps echoed down the hallway behind him, and a moment later, she came around to face him. With a sigh, he opened his eyes to meet her gaze.

"Let's talk." She glanced down the hallway behind him, presumably to make sure Adrian wasn't following, then ushered him around the corner and down another hall, her steps frantic as she led him away.

"I'm not sure I want to." But he still followed her, powerless to resist.

She opened a door and let out a sigh of relief as it turned out to be a small reception room. They entered, and she closed the door behind them, leaning against it. Preston walked into the middle of the room before turning back to look at her.

"I don't want your pity," he said when she opened her mouth to speak, hating how raw his voice sounded. "Don't give me platitudes about how I will find someone else. I have no interest in anyone else. And also, I'm a grown man and I will get over this given time."

Even as he said the words, he knew they were a lie—he wasn't sure he'd ever get over her.

Her brow furrowed as she looked at him. "So you really do love me?"

"Bloody hell, Amelia!" He threw his arms out in frustration. "Why do you think I've been telling you I do?"

"I..." She made a small grimace. "I thought you were doing it out of some misguided honour after kissing me. Since you've been very clear about not wanting to risk my reputation."

He stared at her for a moment, then chuckled, despite his heart aching like it was being pierced by a thousand needles. "Hell. Amelia, I'm not *that* honourable. Like you enjoy reminding me, I *am* a rake."

And, apparently, a fool.

"A rake who claims he would never ruin anyone. And yet you have been quite close to ruining me," she pointed out.

A grin spread across his face at her sweet innocence. "Sweetheart, while those were some amazing kisses that would definitely have ruined your reputation had someone found out... That was far from ruining you."

"Oh?" A glint of curiosity sparked to life in her eyes. "I must admit to knowing very little of the final act. No one will tell me. They all say I will find out once I'm married. I assumed kissing was a significant part of it, considering how scandalous it is for an unmarried woman to kiss someone."

This was not a conversation he ought to have with the woman who had practically just rejected his suit. And yet, he could not stay away. His feet moved of their own volition, bringing him closer to her, where she remained at the door. "There's quite a lot more to it."

Tilting her head to the side, she looked at him. "Such as?"

He groaned but couldn't make himself retreat. "Amelia... I really should not speak to you of such things."

"Why not?" she grumbled. "No one else will. How will I know what to avoid if no one will tell me?"

Unable to resist her allure, he took the few steps separating them, coming to stand in front of her. She tilted her head to look up at him, and he wished he knew what she was thinking. What she wanted.

No matter what, she was making no effort to move away from him, and his heart skipped a beat. He lifted his hand to trace her bottom lip with the pad of his thumb, his eyes following the movement. She had a beautiful mouth. Soft and full, with a marked bow.

"You'd do well to stay away from all of it," he mumbled, even as his other hand came up to rest on her waist. He wanted to pull her close, to show her exactly what she should avoid, but that would be madness. Why was he punishing himself? He was only prolonging his torment. But he could not pull away from her. Not when her soft lips opened on a shaky breath, the hot air brushing over his knuckles.

Her eyes met his, and as he pulled his hand back, her tongue darted out to wet her lips. A rush of desire went straight to his groin. Damn, he should have stayed on the other side of the room.

"'*All of it*' is rather vague, don't you think?" Her voice was barely a whisper.

He cocked a brow at her question. She was challenging him. Taunting him. He should not raise to the bait. He knew better. *She* knew better. This was a dangerous game they were playing.

Knowing he would do better to leave the room, he lowered his head until their noses nearly touched. His body hummed with awareness of her, every instinct screaming at him to kiss her, even as his mind warned him away.

"Would you like a demonstration?"

Chapter Fourteen

Amelia's mouth was dry as she met the challenge in Preston's green eyes. If there was ever a time she should run away from him, this was it. She had a plan, and he was not part of it, and yet... She inclined her head in a barely perceptible nod.

Something dark and dangerous glittered in his eyes, stirring the fluttering inside her abdomen once again.

"For a start," he mumbled as his knuckles dropped to the bare skin on her shoulder next to the collar line of her dress, "never allow a man this close to you. It is far too scandalous and allows him far too much freedom."

Using his fingertips, he trailed a path along the fabric of her dress, chasing gooseflesh across her chest, his touch deliberate and teasing. Reaching the opposite shoulder, he followed the line of her clavicles to return to his original position. Anticipation of his next move kept her grounded to the spot, unable to move, as he hesitated.

Was he waiting for her to tell him to stop? She had no inclination to do so. In fact, she wanted quite the opposite—she wanted more, even though she knew she shouldn't.

When she remained silent, he raised a dark brow before leaning down. As his hot breath fanned her neck, she placed her palms against the flat surface of the door behind her to keep herself from reaching for him. His lips dragged across the sensitive spot below her ear, making her draw a sharp breath as the butterflies in her abdomen exploded in a flurry of fluttering wings.

Reaching the area where her neck met her shoulder, he kissed it, his warm lips against her skin sending tingles throughout her entire being.

"Definitely don't allow anyone to do this," he mumbled against her, and she had to bite her lower lip to keep silent when he continued lavishing her neck with hot kisses and gentle nibbles. When he teased her earlobe with his tongue, she couldn't hold back the low moan that wrenched free of her throat, her body reacting to his touch with a ferocity that terrified her.

Preston pulled back slightly, drawing a deep breath.

"Bloody hell." The hoarse quality of his voice sent a pleasurable shiver down her spine to pool low in her abdomen.

The hand at her waist grabbed a fistful of fabric from her dress in a tight grip, as if he struggled to hold back. The possibility of that made her giddy. He might not be who she envisioned for a husband, but the thought of bringing a rake of his calibre to his knees was not without merit. She could admit to being vain enough to appreciate the idea of him unable to resist her.

"What else?" she asked quietly, her voice trembling every so slightly. "I need to know what to look out for."

The dark chuckle against her neck reverberated through her body. Lifting his head, Preston looked down at her. "Are you trying to break me, Amelia?"

"In what way?"

The corners of his mouth curved into a wry smile. "Every way."

She pursed her lips. "I haven't considered. If I'm honest, not much planning has gone into this."

"One would hope," he muttered, but there was an amused glint in his eyes.

When he did nothing, she shifted from one foot to the other. After another moment of nothing, she cleared her throat. "So, are you going to continue?"

His gaze swept over her, his eyes hooded. "I really ought to leave before we do something we regret."

He was clearly trying to be the voice of reason, but she didn't want to be reasonable. Not right now. She cocked her head to the side. "Do you regret kissing me?"

With a groan, he dragged a hand through his dark hair. "Yes, and no."

"Oh." Why was she disappointed? She tapped her fingers against the door behind her as she tried to figure out her complicated feelings. She wanted Preston to kiss her. Wanted him to *want* to kiss her. Even if he was everything she should not want. "Did you not enjoy it?"

"Amelia, I absolutely enjoyed kissing you. Probably too much. But now that I've tasted you..." He cleared his throat, his gaze lingering on her lips for a moment too long. Shaking his head, he smiled wryly. "I don't want to stop. If I had never kissed you... At least I wouldn't know exactly what I was missing."

Guilt washed over her. She didn't mean to be playing with his feelings. It was unfair of her to keep coming back to him after he had admitted how he felt. Especially now that she knew he had meant it.

Originally, she had truly believed he only said it out of some misguided honour, but she believed him now, could no longer deny his feelings. Nor could she deny being attracted to him. If he wasn't a rake, she probably would not have hesitated to accept his suit. But she did not subscribe to the idea that reformed rakes made the best husbands. She rather doubted they could ever truly be reformed. And she could not risk it—would not risk it.

She had no intention of ever entrusting a rake with her heart again. And she suspected that if Preston broke her heart, she would never recover. This was nothing like the youthful infatuation she'd had with Fulmer. What she felt for Preston was much bigger, and much more dangerous. Which was exactly why she ought to leave this room right this minute. Only her feet refused to move.

As if he had a similar thought, Preston sighed. "You should leave. If anyone finds us, it would be a scandal."

It would. They'd be forced to marry. But she still wasn't moving. Her body still tingled from his earlier touches, and she wasn't ready to relinquish that feeling. He stood close enough that she could feel the heat radiating from his body, the pull to walk into his embrace almost overwhelming. If only she had developed these feelings for someone else. This unbearable attraction.

It was selfish of her, but she could not stop herself from putting a hand on his chest. He glanced down at it, the stark contrast between her white glove against his black tailcoat, before meeting her gaze.

"Amelia?" There were so many questions in that one word, but she had no answers. Just knew she wasn't ready to let him go. Not ready for this moment to be over.

"You have not finished your instructions," she said quietly. "I still don't fully know what to avoid."

Preston closed his eyes for a moment. "You will be the end of me," he mumbled, then chuckled. "And not only because your brothers would be as likely to shoot me as anything else if they found us."

She giggled, the sound a little more nervous than she'd like. "They are really against this match."

He sobered and stared down at her. "So are you."

Meeting his gaze, she wasn't sure she was as against it as she ought to be. Except for his rakishness, Preston was pretty much everything she wanted in a husband. Caring and attentive. Always close to a smile. And he made her laugh. She loved their teasing discussions.

But she would not fall in love with him. It just was not an option. Which was exactly why she should leave right now. Before she pulled his head down for the kiss she had been longing for all day.

"I'm sorry," she blurted before turning around and opening the door. Before she could change her mind. Before she could give in to her heart. Leaving Preston behind, she left the room and walked back towards the ballroom.

Poor Preston. She was forever running away from him.

Not wishing to speak to anyone, she slipped out onto the terrace only to run into another woman who dropped her fan from the impact. She really must start paying more attention. This was not the first time she'd walked straight into someone while her mind was too preoccupied with thoughts of Preston.

"My apologies!" she said quickly, as she bent to retrieve the fan. Handing it back to the woman, she recognised the blonde as Viscount Gowthorpe's sister whose coming-out ball she was attending. They had been introduced earlier in the evening. "Miss Grafton? Are you all right?"

The young woman smiled, even if it did not quite reach her eyes. Maybe she had been planning to hide on the terrace as well. "I am fine, thank you, Lady Amelia. I hope you're enjoying the ball?"

Amelia threw a look over her shoulder to make sure Preston or her brother had not followed her, desperate for a moment without men confusing her thoughts. "Yes, thank you. It is a lovely ball." Turning back to the other woman, she smiled wryly. "Though I must admit, I am hiding for a moment."

Miss Grafton laughed quietly. "I can appreciate the need for a moment alone. In truth, I often sneak outside during balls and events for a brief respite from the crowds."

"They can be rather stifling, can they not?" Amelia grinned, enjoying the other woman's candour.

"Quite."

"Would you care to stay out here with me for a moment? No gentleman will approach us if we appear deep in discussion. Or so I hope."

"I'd love to." Miss Grafton nodded, and they walked over to stand by the terrace railing looking out over the garden.

Amelia had no intention of venturing into the garden tonight. Whenever she did, she appeared to do something foolish. Like kissing Preston. She groaned inwardly as the mere thought made her insides flutter to life.

"Is something the matter?" Miss Grafton asked, her voice soft and kind.

"No." Amelia sighed, her gaze fixed on her hands. "Maybe? I am trying to make sense of this whole courtship thing. Of love."

She had never thought her life would be quite so complicated. Love quite so elusive. Or Preston quite so... tempting.

"Oh." The young woman smiled. "I know very little of such things. My family has intended for me to marry a gentleman already chosen for me since I was still a child."

"It is not as if they explain anything to us anyway," Amelia muttered. "All I know is that this man is all wrong for me."

Her cheeks heated as she realised she'd said too much. Miss Grafton said nothing at first, only stared out over the garden with a line between her brows as she considered the statement. Almost as if she knew exactly what Amelia was talking about.

"Please ignore my ramblings," Amelia said. "I have a tendency to speak too freely."

Miss Grafton turned her head to meet her gaze. "Never apologise. It's a fresh breath in a society where everyone is forever polite. Forever holding back what they truly wish to say."

Amelia laughed. "Not I. To my family's frustration, I imagine."

"The only thing I know with certainty about love," Miss Grafton said thoughtfully, "is that we cannot choose who we feel for. Nor can we force feelings for someone. No matter how much we might try."

"Well, that is not good enough," Amelia complained. "I should be able to choose who I care for. There should be a list of requirements, and if they do not meet them, then I should not be able to fall for them."

"If only it were so." Miss Grafton sighed. "Life would certainly be much easier if we could choose like that."

The wistful note in the other woman's voice piqued Amelia's interest, but she didn't want to pry. No, she definitely wanted to pry, but she didn't know the young lady well enough yet to do so.

"So what do we do?" she asked, unsure of whether she was asking herself or Miss Grafton. "If we are doomed to follow the whims of our emotions?"

"We do what we can, I suppose." Miss Grafton lifted her head to the pale moon hanging above the garden. "Does your gentleman share your feelings?"

"I…" Amelia looked down at her hands, her fingers tapping against the stone railing. Why was she pouring her heart out to this stranger? They had only met today. And yet, she felt as if her secrets would be safe, and it felt good to speak to someone about her tumultuous thoughts. "He said he loves me."

Saying it out loud felt strange. Like it somehow made it more real. Confirmed his admission.

"Do you love him? You said he is wrong for you, but how do you feel about him?" Miss Grafton's voice was so gentle, so kind, that Amelia had to hold herself back from blurting out every little thought and all of her confused feelings she had about Preston.

Scowling at nothing in particular, she thought about him. About his wry smiles that made her insides lurch. About his easy conversation that always entertained her. About his kisses that made her head spin, and her body ache for more.

"How do I know? How do I know if it's only attraction or something more?"

"Well..." Miss Grafton hedged. "Can you imagine your life without him? Can you imagine him married to someone else?"

The idea of Preston with another woman made her queasy. And a life without him? She had never imagined such a thing. He had been a constant in hers for as long as she could remember, so a life without him simply did not exist, and the thought of it made her heart ache. Her eyes widened as the truth hit her like a physical blow.

Blast! She did love him. Had probably loved him for longer than she cared to admit.

She buried her face in her gloved hands, her pulse racing as the truth washed over her. "But what do you do if he's not what you wanted? I swore to stay away from rakes."

Miss Grafton smiled, her eyes warm with understanding. "I believe anyone is capable of change. Maybe you need to give him the chance to prove to you that he can."

Amelia chuckled. "How are you so positive?"

The other woman lifted a shoulder in a shrug. "I have to be. Life is too bleak without a positive outlook."

"Thank you for this chat," Amelia said, and she truly meant it. Walking to the doors to the ballroom, she stopped and turned around. "I wish you luck with your situation, too. I hope you find every happiness."

A shadow passed over Miss Grafton's face, but she smiled and nodded. "Thank you. You too."

Turning back to the doors, Amelia almost bumped into the Marquess of Pensington. Again. She really must learn to look before walking.

She curtsied. "My lord."

"Lady Amelia," he said as he sketched a bow.

She didn't stay to see if he would make conversation. She needed to see Preston, and she needed to see him now. It was time to stop running and tell him the truth. That she had no future, no life, without him. That despite all her protests about rakes, all her carefully laid plans, her heart had chosen him anyway.

Chapter Fifteen

Preston sat alone in his library nursing a glass of brandy, the bitter taste matching his mood. Never had rejection stung quite like this. He was feeling rather sorry for himself when the door opened behind him. Comfortable in his chair, staring out over the dark garden outside, he didn't bother turning around.

"It's all right, Giles," he said, waving a hand at the butler. "You can tell the valet to go to bed. I will sort myself out, as I don't know when I will retire for the night."

Someone cleared their throat, making him frown. That didn't sound like his butler.

"I'm afraid Giles can't deliver your message." The soft voice was like a caress against his skin, and his breath hitched at the sound of it, even as his mind warned him this was dangerous territory.

With his heart in his throat, he stood and turned to the interloper. "Amelia," he said, keeping his voice measured despite his racing pulse. "What are you doing here? It's the middle of the night. Have you no sense of propriety?"

She wore a large cloak covering most of her form, but he could see the ball dress from earlier in the evening underneath it. "Apparently not," she replied. "I wanted... No, I *needed* to speak to you. And you had already left Gowthorpe's ball."

Walking around the desk to lean back against it, he shook his head. "What could possibly be so important that you risk your reputation by visiting me alone at night?" He made a show of looking behind her. "I see you have no chaperone. How did you even get inside?"

"I left my maid at home," she admitted with a lack of concern that should frustrate him, but despite everything, he was happy to see her. Why had she come? A flicker of hope fluttered to life in his chest, no matter how hard he tried to extinguish it. "And I snuck in through the servants' entrance in the back."

He took a sip of his drink as he watched her, trying to determine her purpose for this improper visit. Setting the glass down on the desk behind him, he crossed his arms over his chest. "And why, pray tell, have you decided to visit me at this hour?"

"I... I needed to speak with you." With lightly trembling fingers, she untied the cloak and slid it off before throwing it on a chair.

He frowned. A nervous Amelia? That was not a common sight. "Yes," he said. "You mentioned that already. What was so important it couldn't wait until tomorrow?"

Instead of answering him straight away, she paced the room from side to side, not unlike the time she had come to him to request his help with capturing the interest of the Marquess of Pensington.

Not sure what to expect, he remained half-sitting on his desk as he watched her continue to tread a path across the floor of his library. A few strands of hair had come loose from her intricate hairdo to caress the curves of her neck and shoulders. Pushing it back behind her ears, she let out a frustrated huff before she stopped to level him with a glare.

"You're all wrong!" she burst out.

"So you've told me," he drawled.

"I have no interest in rakes. A rake is exactly what I don't want. Shouldn't want." She took a few steps towards him, making him straighten. "But a friend pointed something out to me tonight…"

"And what's that?" He swallowed as she took the remaining steps separating them, coming to stand in front of him.

Refusing to meet his gaze, she kept her eyes trained on the buttons on his shirt where he'd removed his cravat after returning home. "She said you can't choose who you love."

His heart beat rapidly in his chest as he waited for her to elaborate.

She sighed. "I already know I'm attracted to you." A wry smile touched her lips. "We both do. But I refused to believe it was anything beyond that. Because how could I fall in love with exactly the type of man I do not want?"

"Because we don't get to choose who we love any more than we can choose who we are attracted to?" he ventured a quiet guess.

"Exactly." Her head slowly tilted until her brown eyes met his, and he saw something in them he'd never dared hope to see. "You may be exactly what I don't want. But you are also everything I do want. You make me laugh. You talk to me like my opinion matters. I..." She faltered, her cheeks turning pink under his intense scrutiny. "I love you, Preston."

Her words struck him like a punch to the gut, stealing his breath away. Unable to resist any longer, he pulled her to him and pressed his mouth to hers. When her lips opened in surprise, he took immediate advantage and deepened the kiss. Savouring every moment of her in his arms. She melted into his embrace with a happy sigh, and her arms slid around his shoulders to bury in the hair at the back of his head.

He wanted her in his life. Every day. He wanted to wake up every morning and go to sleep every night with her next to him. He wanted to talk to her and laugh with her. Other than her brother, she was his best friend, and he would do anything to make her happy.

But right this moment... Right now, he wanted nothing more than to keep kissing her. To taste every inch of her body and hear her cry out his name as she came apart in his arms.

Dragging his lips down her neck, he licked and nibbled, every sound, every moan spurring him on further. His hands slid down to grip her hips, allowing him to swing her around and lift her up to sit on the edge of the desk.

He wedged between her knees as her legs parted, while returning to capture her mouth in a passionate kiss. Amelia responded to his every move with equal fervour. Bunching the skirt of her dress in his hand, he slowly pulled it up her legs until he could feel the bare skin above her stockings.

It was so very tempting to move his hand further up. To seek her heat, but he forced himself to pull back slightly. His hesitation made her shift restlessly on the desk, her hands pulling lightly on his shirt collar to bring his mouth back to hers.

"Amelia," he whispered, his voice hoarse with desire. "We must stop before I prove myself every bit the rake you accuse me of being. The side of me I am trying to leave behind."

Her eyes fluttered open and her hands lowered to her lap. "You are?"

He nodded. "I have not been with another woman since the moment I realised I loved you."

When her tongue darted out to wet her lips, he nearly captured her mouth in another kiss, but held back. Barely.

"And how long ago is that?" she asked.

"When you came out for your first season. It became rather obvious when I was jealous of every man courting you. Every smile you bestowed on someone who was not me. Every dance shared with someone else." The memories of watching her from afar, of pretending indifference while his heart ached, were still painfully fresh.

"That is more than a year ago!" Her eyes widened, and she nudged his chest teasingly. "You have known all this time, and you never told me!"

The corners of his mouth curved into a self-deprecating smile. "I know that I'm not quite what you want. Or deserve. I had planned to take the secret of my love for you to my grave. Then you came to me with your scheme to trap Pensington... and I could not stay away from you."

She grinned. "I'm glad you could not."

Leaning down, he buried his nose in the hair at her temple, taking in the faint flowery smell. "So am I," he admitted.

Unable to withstand the temptation any longer, he placed a kiss on the sensitive spot below her ear. She let out a shuddering breath as he dragged his lips down along her neck, tasting her skin. The sound rekindled his desire instantly, and his hand slid along the contours of her waist and hip, desperately wanting to pull her closer.

"Your brothers will not approve," he mumbled against her shoulder.

"Perhaps not," she agreed. "So let's not give them the chance to."

He raised his head to look at her, unsure of what she was suggesting.

She smiled slowly, a wicked glint in her brown eyes. "Tonight," she said. "Be a rake. Make sure my brothers have no recourse other than to see us married."

The words hung between them, heavy with implications, with promise.

When he didn't immediately answer—he wasn't sure he remembered how to use words right then—she put her hand on his chest just above his heart, and her eyes met his. In them, he saw not just desire, but trust. Complete and absolute trust.

"Seduce me, Preston."

Chapter Sixteen

Amelia's heart beat painfully against her ribs as she waited for Preston's answer to her scandalous suggestion. His hand at her waist flexed, but he said nothing, and the silence was almost unbearable. Why was he not responding?

"Preston?"

His mouth crashed into hers, and he pulled her into his arms, his kiss urgent and passionate as he devoured her. Excitement flared inside her. This was it. If they went through with this plan, there was no going back. She should be worried about losing her innocence, but she wasn't. Preston might have been a rake before, but said he had given up that life once he realised he wanted her. If that wasn't proof he was worth taking a chance on, she wasn't sure what was.

"We cannot stay here." He raised his head and placed a soft kiss on her cheek before lifting her off the desk and taking her hand, his fingers lacing through hers as if he was scared to let her go.

"Where are we going?" Her breath came in short bursts, her heart pounding. This was both frightening and exhilarating.

Soon she would know what the married ladies of her acquaintance were whispering about when they thought she couldn't hear. Some things she'd overheard made it sound like a man's attentions were the last thing she should want, but so far, everything Preston had done with her had been sinfully enjoyable.

He pulled her along out of the library and down a hallway. When he looked back at her and grinned wickedly, her stomach did an awkward somersault.

"To my bedchamber."

They reached his upstairs bedchamber not long after, and when he closed the door behind them, she shivered. This was incredibly exciting. And maybe just a touch daunting. She was, after all, hopelessly inexperienced in these things.

And here she was, in Preston's home, in his private space, about to give herself to him, and her life would never be the same. But rather than fear, she felt only certainty. This was right. *He* was right.

He moved ahead of her, lighting a few candles to assist the fire in the grate in illuminating the room. Even with the candles, it was difficult to see details properly without daylight pouring in through the windows. From what she could tell, the walls were a deep green, while decorative cushions and fabrics were mostly a rich marigold. A large four-poster bed opposite the fireplace drew her eyes to it, and she quickly forgot about any other piece of furniture.

"Have you changed your mind?" His voice was soft, filled with a concern that did little to soothe her frayed nerves.

She nearly jumped as he came up next to her, his hand rubbing her upper arm. "No, but I would lie if I did not admit to finding it a little frightening." Looking up at his loving face, she smiled wryly. "I have never done this."

His hand on her arm slid down to capture her hand, and he lifted it to his lips for a kiss. "You know, we could simply *say* that I have compromised you. I hardly think your brothers would question it."

"We could," she allowed. "But I don't want to leave."

"Then we'll go slow." Still holding her hand, he used his other one to loosen the fingers of her glove before sliding it off, his touch gentle. Finally being skin to skin, he turned her hand over and placed a kiss in her palm. The light stubble on his chin tickled, and the touch sent a jolt of awareness up her arm. "If at any time you want me to stop, just say so."

She nodded. Or at least she thought she did. Every cell in her body was on edge, fully focused on every little thing he did. The gentle tug as he pulled off her other glove. His hands on her shoulders as he turned her towards the fireplace and he stood behind her to unbutton the back of her gown. Warm lips against the shell of her ear as the fabric fell to the floor at her feet.

Sliding his hands along the side of her chest and waist, he placed a teasing kiss below her ear, and his hot breath fanned her neck. She shuddered when he continued kissing and nibbling on her neck as he unhurriedly unlaced her stays. As soon as the garment joined her dress on the floor, he stepped closer, bringing her back against his tall frame.

His arm moved around her waist, warm even through the remaining layer of her thin shift. The only thing she was still wearing other than her slippers and stockings. Her body tingled with anticipation of what might come next. He cupped her breast through the fabric, and her eyes fluttered closed as he gently massaged her. When his thumb flicked across her nipple, she gasped as another jolt shocked her.

She moved restlessly against him, and he groaned as something hard pressed against the curve of her bottom. What was that? Curious, she turned around and slid her hand over the front of his breeches. He immediately sucked in a breath, and her gaze sought his.

"Did I hurt you?"

He shook his head.

"What is that?"

He stared at her for a moment. Taking a step away, he swore softly. "Damn, I didn't realise quite how innocent you are. I thought perhaps you knew some of what goes on between a man and a woman."

Crossing her arms over her chest, she gave him an annoyed look. "I told you I don't. No one will tell me anything."

"Well, I..." He cleared his throat. Ran a hand through his hair. Shifted from one leg to the other. "Men and women are created differently," he finally said. His cheeks stained pink as he muttered, "Hell. I can see why this is something mothers are meant to do."

"Oh." She pursed her lips as she considered his words. "Like animals?"

"Yes!" he latched on to her words with renewed vigour. "Your family has dogs and horses. Have you ever seen them mate?"

"My family usually keeps me away from such things, but I came across it once," she admitted. Her eyes widened. "Is that what we are meant to do?"

He chuckled at her apparent shock. "Not quite. But sort of?"

Without meaning to, her eyes strayed from his face to the bulge in his breeches. She frowned. "It's not the same as horses, right?"

A laugh escaped him. "No. Fear not, the..." He chuckled again. "The size is much more reasonable."

She certainly hoped so because it certainly had not felt tiny against her hand. Nervous excitement coursed through her at the prospect of what lay ahead. It was difficult to imagine exactly what that was, but every touch from Preston confirmed that this was the right choice. This was what she wanted. He was what she wanted.

Regaining some of her confidence, she gave him a teasing smile. "I feel you are far too overdressed for this. I am nearly completely undressed while you only lack your cravat."

The corners of his mouth twitched. "And what would you suggest I do about this?"

With a sultry glance at him, she sauntered over to his bed, imagining his eyes following her every step. She kicked off her slippers before turning around and sitting down on the bed. Waving her hand gracefully, as if giving him leave, she nodded towards him. "Go ahead. Undress."

A grin spread over his handsome face, and she noted that his eyes were dark with desire as he watched her. "As you command, love."

He shrugged out of his black tailcoat, unbuttoned his waistcoat and took it off, then pulled his shirt over his head. The teasing smile faded from her lips as she took in the shape of his half-naked form. He was tall and lean, his shoulders wide with narrow hips.

The warm light of the fire in the grate and candles played across his skin, emphasising the flat stomach and well-defined upper chest. It looked nothing like her own, and her fingers itched to touch him. Explore him.

"Keep going," she said when he didn't continue, her voice little more than a whisper.

"I'll keep my breeches on for now. I don't want to see you fleeing the room." He winked.

She giggled. "Are you saying I would be so frightened by what I see that I would bolt?"

He removed his shoes before giving her a dark look that made her stomach lurch awkwardly. "I certainly hope not. However,"—he stalked towards her, his eyes not leaving her—"I'm not willing to take the chance. As you said, this is all new to you, and I can only imagine it might be overwhelming."

When he stopped in front of her, she tilted her head back to look up at him. "True. I can't quite fathom how this will work. From what little I've overheard, the woman is meant to lie still and endure."

A small laugh escaped him. "I certainly hope I can do more than have you *endure*."

Her cheeks heated. "I have enjoyed everything until now, so I can't imagine it turning too horrible."

"Let's hope not," he mumbled, his hand coming up to cup her face.

He was so close she could smell the light scent of whichever soap he favoured. Something spicy that tickled her nose. Unable to resist any longer, she raised a hand and placed it on his abdomen. The muscles tensed under her palm as she moved over his skin, revelling in the feeling. He was hard where she was soft. Flat where she had curves.

It was with remarkable patience Preston allowed her to explore every inch of him, and she appreciated that he didn't make her feel hurried. But when she returned to trace the dark shape in his breeches, he soon caught her hand in his. Lifting her gaze to ask him why, he simply shook his head.

"Not yet, love. There is a limit to how much of your touch I can withstand." He smiled warmly to soften his words.

She nodded. Part of her wanted to ask him to remove his breeches. The other part was a little scared of what she would see. For now, the latter won.

Bending down, Preston caught her mouth in a searing kiss. She scooted back on the bed, and he followed, his lips not leaving hers, and as she came to rest against the pillows at the head, he half-covered her body with his. The nearness was intoxicating. His tongue stole across her lips to deepen the kiss, stoking her desire higher with every stroke. Heat gathered at the junction of her thighs and she wriggled against him. She wanted more, even if she wasn't entirely sure what that more was.

One of his hands caressed her leg from below her knee and up along her thigh, pushing her thin shift along with it. When his fingertips reached the bare skin above her stockings, she gasped as another jolt reverberated through her. His mouth dropped to her shoulder, kissing her neck, while his fingers trailed over her sensitive skin until they finally reached her heated core.

The touch was so personal, so intimate, that she buried her face in his shoulder, relieved he couldn't see her burning face. She moaned as he caressed her, his touch evoking pleasures she had never experienced before. When he found her most sensitive spot and rubbed gently, she nearly bounced off the bed. Fire travelled from his touch through every inch of her body, setting every part of her ablaze.

"P... Preston," she gasped. "I can't... I don't know..."

His touch stilled for a moment, letting her catch her breath, even if his hand remained between her legs. Lifting his head, he pressed a quick, fervent kiss to her lips. "Amelia," he mumbled, his voice hoarse. "You are amazing. I love touching you. But if you want to stop, just say the word."

Stopping was the furthest thing from her mind. She wound her arms around his neck and pulled him down for another kiss. "No," she said. "I'm worried I feel too much. Is... is this normal? I feel like I might explode."

He groaned. "Yes, that's exactly how it should feel." A smile broke through on his lips. "As long as I'm doing things right."

Could her cheeks get any hotter? She doubted it. "I'm fairly confident you are," she muttered self-consciously. "I didn't think ladies were meant to enjoy it this much."

"The best ladies do," he promised, making her gasp as he moved his hand again. Kissing her neck, he dragged his mouth higher, his hot breath fanning her ear. "Let's see if I can make it even better..."

She didn't have time to ask what he was referring to before she felt his finger tease her opening, now slick with desire. When his thumb rubbed at her sensitive spot, she moaned as the fire instantly roared to life again. His other finger slipped inside her, the intrusion a strange sensation, but far from unpleasant.

"Preston!" she gasped, but she wasn't even sure what she was asking for. Every stroke, every flick of his thumb brought her closer to the brink. Her body was aflame, burning hotly under his touch.

"Amelia," he mumbled against her ear. "Don't hold back."

He increased the pace and pressure of his caresses slightly, and a moment later her world exploded with blinding light as she cried out his name.

When her breathing finally slowed down, he gathered her in his arms and kissed her. She closed her eyes and enjoyed the warmth enveloping her.

"Am I compromised now?" she asked as she fought a yawn.

His quiet chuckle reverberated through her. "Technically? No. But in every way that your brothers care about? Probably."

In the heat of the moment, she had forgotten the fact that he still wore his breeches. From what little she had seen when walking in on the horses mating, they had missed a crucial step. The final, irrevocable step. The step she desperately wanted, even after what she had just experienced.

Raising herself up on her elbow, she looked down at Preston. He looked surprisingly relaxed for someone who had just nearly compromised a duke's daughter. Noticing her movement, he opened one eye to peer at her.

"Not good enough," she said, making him open the other eye too to stare at her with his eyebrows raised. "I want to be thoroughly compromised. No half measures."

"Is that so?" he asked lazily, and she nodded.

A gasp escaped her as he grabbed her and flipped her over onto her back. When he moved on top of her, she automatically spread her knees to accommodate his hips between her legs. He still wore his breeches, but even with the layer of fabric between them, she could feel the hardness against her heat. He pressed a quick, fervent kiss on her lips before smiling wickedly.

"I'll have you know," he said, his dark voice making her shiver, "I put effort into this. But if my performance was not to your standards, I will have to try harder."

As if to prove his point, he rocked his hips and the delicious friction against her set off a burst of pleasure that tore a moan from her lips.

"Y... Yes. Try harder." She gasped as he did just that, rubbing against her and re-awakening the desire she had thought vaporised in her earlier climax. Apparently not, as it came back in full force, increasing with every move of his hips.

He stopped for a moment, and she almost admonished him, until he quickly helped her out of her shift. As she lay naked before him, wearing nothing but her stockings, he gazed down on her and the love in his eyes banished any embarrassment about being so exposed.

"You're beautiful," he breathed. His eyes came back to hers. "Are you certain this is what you want, Amelia? We can always lie to your brothers and say you're fully compromised."

Reaching her hand up to caress his cheek, she nodded. "Yes, I'm certain, Preston. I love you, and I truly want this. I want you. Now."

He groaned at her words. Raising himself up on his knees, he held her gaze as he began unbuttoning his breeches. She swallowed, both excited and curious. As he pushed his breeches off and wriggled out of them, she couldn't keep her eyes from straying to the erect part of him that strained towards her. *Oh my.* Her mouth felt dry, and she might have worried about the logistics of everything had Preston not leaned down and kissed her passionately.

His hand cupped her breast and teased her nipple to a hard point, leaving her gasping in his arms. Heat gathered between her thighs, but it felt as if something was missing. She wanted Preston closer. So much closer. A moan tore from her lips as he dipped his head to capture a nipple in his mouth, sucking and licking until she squirmed in his arms.

"I want more," she whispered. Her hands pulled on him as if she could somehow bring him closer by sheer willpower.

His mouth found hers again, and his hips settled back between her legs, his hardness pressing against her, rubbing against that most sensitive spot. The slow, drugging kisses matched the movements of his hips, increasing her pleasure with every stroke. Finally, he tore his mouth from hers, his breathing heavy.

"This... This might hurt," he admitted. "I've heard it can the first time."

They'd made it this far, and she wasn't about to back down now, so she shifted against him and was rewarded by a small moan. "No turning back now," she said.

He kissed her again, and a moment later she felt some pressure as he pushed into her. It was an odd sensation, similar to when he had used his finger, and yet completely different. But it didn't hurt. Her body craved this. They had spent so long this evening stirring her desire that now she didn't want to wait any longer. When he didn't immediately move, she shifted against him again.

Leaning his head against her shoulder, he groaned against her skin. "Amelia," he said, his voice slightly muffled. "I'm trying to take it slow. Please don't move, I'm—"

He moaned as she squirmed underneath him.

"Don't take it slow. I want you, Preston." She trailed her fingertips down along his back, and he cursed softly.

It was her turn to moan as he pulled back slightly before pushing back inside her, deeper this time. He continued, every move of his hips bringing her more pleasure. More heat. His lips found the sensitive spot on her neck and he kissed, sucked and nibbled as he continued his passionate onslaught.

With his hands, he grabbed her hips and angled them slightly, allowing him to reach a spot that increased her pleasure further. The explosion came quicker this time, as if her body knew what to expect now. Preston followed closely behind, increasing his pace before burying himself deep inside her with a groan, before collapsing on her.

Placing a kiss on his temple, she whispered. "I love you."

She could feel his smile against the skin of her shoulder. "I love you too," he mumbled.

Rolling off her, he pulled her close, and she settled into his embrace as if it was something they had always done. It felt right. This was where she was meant to be. In Preston's arms.

Chapter Seventeen

"You did *what*?" Even Richmond's usually tempered voice rose as he stood behind his desk, leaning forward with his hands against the wooden surface. "Please tell me I heard you incorrectly."

Telling Amelia's brothers was going about as well as Preston had imagined. Adrian didn't bother with questions. He was already striding across the room with his hands in tight fists. The contrast in their reactions was as different as the brothers' personalities. One subdued. One volatile. And somehow, facing them both, Preston found himself more worried about losing his best friend than about physical violence.

"You bastard," Adrian growled as he reached him. "I told you to stay away from her!"

The attack he expected didn't come, and as he met his friend's glare, he almost sighed with relief. Adrian packed one hell of a punch, even when sparring. An angry one might knock one unconscious.

"I would have stayed away," he said slowly, squaring his shoulders under the mutual stares of the Warble brothers. "But I love her and I intend to marry her."

"The hell you are!" Adrian snarled.

Richmond cleared his throat on the other side of the room, making his brother turn to him. "Well, in truth, if he compromised her, Adrian… Then they must marry."

"He's not good enough for her! She deserves better than a rake. Leighton and I are the same, and I could never imagine staying faithful to one woman." Adrian dragged a hand through his dark hair, making it stand on end.

Crossing his arms over his chest, Richmond nodded towards Preston. "Amelia seems to think he's good enough. In the end, that's all that should matter to us. Our sister's wishes and her happiness."

"But how happy will she be when he seeks companionship outside the marriage bed?"

"I would never dishonour Amelia like that," Preston snapped, tired of being spoken about as if he wasn't there. "Yes, I've been a rake in the past, but that life holds no appeal to me now. I put it all behind me the moment I realised I loved Amelia, and I haven't looked at another woman since. I'm surprised you haven't noticed."

Adrian shrugged. "I thought you were in a slump," he muttered.

"If Amelia wants to marry him, and he wants to marry her, then I believe that is the best way forward." Richmond levelled Preston with a sharp look, and Preston realised he'd completely misjudged the man who'd seemed so cold when warning him away from Amelia weeks ago. "But know that if you do anything to jeopardise her happiness, you will face not only Adrian but me as well."

Somehow, the idea of Richmond dropping his polite facade in favour of genuine fury was more terrifying than Adrian's instant anger. Preston nodded.

"I will do everything in my power to make her the happiest woman on earth."

Richmond raised a dark eyebrow. "Now, that's maybe taking it too far. Don't promise something you are not capable of. You're still you."

"I did not know you considered yourself a comedian," Preston muttered. He wasn't sure he'd ever heard the other man crack a joke before, and it was rather disconcerting to see the corners of Richmond's mouth twitch.

Adrian looked a lot less amused, with his lips in a thin line. "I cannot believe you are so willing to accept this match, Richmond."

"The decision has been made for us, so why fret about it? Amelia was certain enough of her feelings that she willingly went to his bed. We owe her the courtesy of accepting her decision. Or would you like to be the one telling her 'no'?"

"No." Adrian cursed softly under his breath when he realised his defeat. Preston tried very hard not to look smug, but he wasn't sure he managed.

The door to the study burst open and Amelia swept inside. Dressed in a green walking dress, she was a vision of health and beauty, only just returned from a stroll in Hyde Park with her friends. With her bonnet in her hands, she looked between the three men before she walked into Preston's arms.

"I cannot believe you went to see them on your own," she hissed. "I thought we agreed to do this together."

He smiled and bent his head to place a soft kiss at her temple. "It was something I felt I needed to do alone. Adrian is my friend, and he deserved to hear it from me before we approach your father."

His friend—if he still was that—had flung himself into an upholstered chair where he sullenly glared at them like a petulant child. His brown eyes narrowed as Amelia lifted a hand to touch Preston's face.

"You're still in one piece," she remarked calmly. "I'm pleased."

"Me too," he admitted with a grin.

"Allow me to speak to Father," Richmond said. "He can be… peculiar at times. I know how to handle him. Once I explain the situation, I'm certain he will allow the two of you to marry."

"Thank you, Richmond." Amelia dashed across the room to give her oldest brother a hug. His eyes widened for a moment, then he relaxed and his arms came up to hug her back.

"As long you are sure this is what you want?"

She pulled back to beam up at him. "It is. I love him."

A rare smile touched Richmond's face. "That's all I wanted to know."

Letting his eyes drift from the siblings to their brother, Preston met Adrian's eyes. The other man shook his head, and getting off the chair, he stalked out of the room, pushing past Preston. With his shoulder smarting from the impact and a knot forming in his stomach, he watched his friend disappear out the door. He truly hoped their friendship was not lost forever.

"He will calm down," Richmond said matter-of-factly. "As long as you keep Amelia happy."

"I hope so."

He smiled down at her as she came back into his arms, hers sneaking around his waist. The warmth of her against him made him feel better. As much as he hoped Adrian would come around, he could not have stayed away from Amelia anymore than he could have stopped breathing. She was his everything. She was his life. He wanted nothing more than to spend every day of his life with her. Seeing her smile and hearing her irresistible laugh.

Richmond cleared his throat. "I will leave the two of you alone. Please try not to get her with child until the wedding."

Amelia's eyes widened and her cheeks glowed pink. "Richmond!"

He winked before leaving them alone. Preston wasn't quite sure what to make of this side of Richmond. Was this the same man who had threatened him to stay away from his sister those weeks ago? Tender fingertips against his face directed his attention back to the woman in his arms. She was looking up at him, her mouth ajar.

"I cannot believe we are getting married," she said slowly. Then she let out a little giggle. "We're getting married, Preston!"

"As soon as your father agrees." He smiled. There was no doubt in his mind Richmond wouldn't be able to convince the duke. He had heard that the older man had taken a step back in recent years, leaving most of the running of the estate to his oldest son. If Richmond recommended the match, the duke would agree.

"I'm sorry Adrian is being such a pain about it." Her lower lip stuck out slightly. "You are his best friend, so he really should be happy for you. Not act like a spoilt child."

He chuckled since he had thought something very similar himself. "There is something special about sisters. Men can get quite protective of them." When she opened her mouth to argue, he continued with a smile. "Not that you cannot take care of yourselves. I'm not saying it's a logical response. But most men like to consider themselves a protector of sorts. So they wish to ensure their sisters' happiness and safety."

She scoffed, but relaxed again. Her brown eyes searched his. "Do you regret it? Us, I mean. If you had not pursued me, the two of you would still be friends."

He shook his head, his heart clenching at the uncertainty in her voice. "I love you. Nothing could keep me from you.

Adrian will come around, but even if he doesn't, you're worth any sacrifice."

A grin touched her lips, and she leaned forward to kiss him. "Good. Because I'm not sure I would have accepted you with anyone else."

His arms around her tightened slightly. No, if given the choice to do it all over again. He would do exactly the same. He would choose Amelia every day. Forever.

Epilogue

Leighton House, Cumberland, England
August 5, 1811

Amelia turned her face towards the warm sun where she lay on a picnic blanket with her head on her husband's arm. The fingers of Preston's other hand played with the hair at her temple, which was oddly relaxing. Her eyes drifted shut as she enjoyed the quiet afternoon on their country estate. The London Season had concluded, and what a season it had been.

A few eyebrows had been raised at their match—mostly because Adrian had accidentally let slip about Preston compromising her during a drunken outburst. While inconvenient, at least it had brought him and Preston back together as he had sheepishly come to apologise for creating the rumour.

At Richmond's behest, they had ignored the whispers, pretending as if it was nothing but malicious gossip. Their wedding had taken place after the customary waiting period while the banns were read. With Amelia being a duke's daughter, no one dared to question them. And if anyone had, she was fairly certain her oldest brother's scowl had quickly stymied their words.

A lavish wedding at the end of June had silenced even the most persistent of gossips as no one could question the love the bride and groom had for each other. In Adrian's words, it had been 'sickening' to watch them stare at each other through the ceremony.

"What are you thinking about?" Preston's smooth voice woke her from her daydreaming, and she opened an eye to peer at him

"Us," she admitted with a smile.

"Only good things, I hope." His fingers drifted from her temple down her face and neck to trace along the decolletage of her dress, making her breath hitch as heat filled her.

"The best." She closed her eyes again as his hand slipped under her dress and stays to cup her breast. Tingles of awareness spread from his touch, slowing her breathing.

"I'll be forever grateful that Pensington never fell for you," Preston mumbled against the sensitive skin on her neck.

"Yes." She struggled to collect her thoughts as he nibbled the spot below her ear. "It's all for the best. Someone else obviously had caught his interest already."

She could feel his smile against her. "Ah, yes. Miss—"

"Please stop manhandling my sister."

The miserable voice made them both jump. Amelia sat up and stared at her brother.

"Adrian," she said. "What are you doing here? We weren't expecting you."

He shrugged before sitting down on the picnic blanket opposite them and stealing a handful of grapes. "Too much attention on me back home with you gone. Mother is nagging a hole through my skull. Saying how I ought to find a wife and settle down. Or find some purpose in life. Join the army. Join the clergy." He groaned. "Can a man not enjoy a leisurely life of doing nothing in peace?"

"Get married," Preston suggested with a sly grin. Then he leaned over and pressed a kiss against Amelia's temple. "It's rather wonderful, I must say."

Adrian scoffed. "No, thank you."

"Then would you mind taking your miserable self elsewhere?" Preston said pointedly. "I was having a rather lovely time with my wife before you interrupted."

Amelia had to hide a smile behind her hand as her brother glared at her husband.

"Is this how you treat guests?"

"It is when they arrive uninvited."

"Fine." Adrian stood, and after brushing his riding breeches off, he sighed. "I will go inside. May I stay for dinner?"

"You may stay as long as you like," Amelia said with a smile. "It's half a day's ride home, so I would never send you away without at least one good night's rest."

He nodded. After a quick bow and the flash of a grin, he disappeared towards the manor house. Amelia leaned into Preston's embrace as she watched her brother's tall form walk across the lawn.

"Do you think we should have told him?"

She could feel Preston's lips curve into a smile against her cheek. "We'll tell him tonight at dinner."

His hand came up to rest on her stomach, the warmth of him heating her even through the layers of her dress. There was hardly a change yet, but as she had not bled since the night he thoroughly compromised her, there could be no doubt about her state.

"Do you think it will be a scandal once people count the weeks and realise the baby is born several too early?" She turned to Preston, but when she saw the love in his eyes, any worries she might have calmed instantly.

"There might be a slight murmur," he admitted. "But the child might simply be a little early, so nothing too bad. Besides," he added. "Your brothers would probably deal with anyone who dares to suggest you were anything but appropriate during our courtship."

"Me?" She giggled. "I was appropriateness personified."

Preston's dark chuckle reverberated through her as he pulled her onto his lap, her legs straddling his hips. "Is that so? I have the distinct memory of a certain young lady appearing in my library and asking me to compromise her."

Her eyes widened in feigned innocence. "I cannot imagine who would be so bold as to do something like that."

"Only someone amazing."

He pulled her head down for a passionate kiss that left her hot and heavy. When she pulled back, her breathing was laboured, and she looked up at the house, half-expecting to see Adrian in the window glaring at them.

"Let's go inside," she murmured. "I don't want my brother to come upon us again."

Preston nodded. Helping her up, he stood and took her hand in his. "Your brother is a dear friend, but he had better not keep interrupting our times together," he warned with a dark look.

"I'm sure he will find something else to occupy him with soon enough." She giggled as her husband pulled her along towards the house.

Life was practically perfect. Preston was practically perfect. She had spent so long looking for the right match when he had been right in front of her all along. All the things she had told herself she wanted—or didn't want—in a husband didn't matter. Because Preston was everything she needed. Everything she wanted. And she'd never been happier.

THE END

www.ingramcontent.com/pod-product-compliance
Lightning Source LLC
LaVergne TN
LVHW041637060526
838200LV00040B/1612